# BLOOD-AXE

## THE SAGA OF A TWENTY-FIRST CENTURY VIKING

## CHRIS J. CLARKE

PENMAN HOUSE
PUBLISHING

ISBN: 0990876497
ISBN- 978-0990876496:

# DEDICATION

This book is dedicated to all those who support OXFAM through donations, volunteer work and on the ground, helping those in desperate need around the world. OXFAM provides emergency relief for famines, droughts and wars, as well as support for longer term projects in health, water supply and much more. It has low management and administration costs.

The charity also conducts research demonstrating how the richest one percent own almost all the world's wealth and a higher proportion of it every year. This builds on the research and extensive evidence provided by Professor Thomas Piketty in his best selling book, "*Capital in the Twenty First Century.*"

As with all my books any profits will be forwarded to OXFAM.

# FOREWORD

Everyone knows of the bloodthirsty, heathen
Vikings. The early Catholic Church made sure of
that. Today, they are seen as representing that
primitive side of human nature that the empathetic
like to think we have defeated.

Sadly, for some activists, destroying statues neither
erases human history nor suppresses humanity's
latent brutishness. On every continent and in all so-
called civilized societies, mankind's inner beast
resurfaces with disturbing regularity.

In the eyes of Christianity, the Vikings were pagan
savages. Papal Propaganda claimed that they had no
civilization. Their sole intent was to burn, rape and
pillage. Of course, when the Crusaders did this, they
said, "It's not the same."

Worst of all, from a Christian perspective, Vikings
desecrated churches and stole or destroyed treasured
holy relics. They tossed the sacred bones of saints
aside and chopped up the reliquaries which
contained them, as hack-silver. They used hack-
silver as money. Most heinous of all, they massacred
Christ's anointed priests in the most horrible ways.

They were the devil's spawn, to be damned for all eternity. This potential fate did not bother the Vikings much at all, until they were eventually converted, ending their version of fun.

During the 8$^{th}$ to the 11$^{th}$ centuries, monasteries were founded throughout what we now call the British Isles, in France and along the European coast, as far away as the Mediterranean. All were vulnerable to raids from the sea or along rivers, at the mercy of the shallow-keeled long-ships, with their fearful dragon heads; full of ruthless warriors from Scandinavia. They called raiding, "going Viking." They could row these vessels through shallow waters. When necessary, they dragged them overland to the next navigable stretch of water on rollers. Once ashore, the Vikings stole horses further enhancing their mobility and opportunities for surprise and plunder.

The monks prayed:

"A facie Nordmannis, liberanos Domine."

(From the fury of the Northmen, O Lord deliver us.)

Their supplications proved ineffective for three-hundred years. Even after that, the complex Norse civilization was not entirely subverted by divine intervention. Over time, the guile of the bishops, desperate to keep and expand collection of their Christian tithes, and to spread their control over the populations and wealth of Europe, finally subverted the old Norse culture. Various Popes sent priests North. They included Pope Sergius III, John X and Agapetus II. To those sent forth, chilly martyrdom probably seemed an attractive alternative to dying of the plague or Leprosy in warmer climes.

Missionaries persuaded the skeptical Norsemen that their tradition of riotous mid-winter parties were suitable for celebrations of the birth of Jesus. Before these times, Christmas was not a feast day. Even today, we have inherited festive fir trees, Yule logs, Wednesday, Thursday, Friday and much else from our North-European ancestors.

\*\*\*

The Norse sagas are poems and stories celebrating deeds of derring-do. They were sung in the halls of the celebrated fierce lords of the sea. Rather than factual history, their intent was to earn the reciters a living, by flattering the lords and to immortalize their fame for future generations. They are difficult to read in our culture, but remember, they had no TV or Internet back in the day. During a drunken celebration, they were likely better received. If your interest is piqued, quaff a few whiskies to enhance our appreciation.

\*\*\*

Those composing and reciting the Norse Sagas were employed by their warlike lords. They wrote to celebrate and embellish deeds and battles. A modern equivalent is the way the Murdoch media only makes positive comments about its rapacious and far-from-perfect paymaster, his friends and his political allies.

The original contributors and audiences for the sagas were the battle-scarred survivors of the bold adventures they retold. Those left behind, shivering in the tenuous safety of their Norse settlements, must have listened in wistful awe.

As Shakespeare put it so well in Henry V's speech before Agincourt,

*"Then will he strip his sleeve and show his scars,*

*And say, 'These wounds I had on Crispin's day.'*

*Old men forget; yet all shall be forgot,*

*But he'll remember, with advantages,*

*What feats he did that day. Then shall our names,*

*Familiar in his mouth as household words....*

*Be in their flowing cups freshly rememb'red.*

*This story shall the good man teach his son."*

\*\*\*

The tattered reputation of Wrong-Way Columbus
has been over-painted and justly so. The Icelandic
saga of Eric the Red and his son Leif Erikson's
landings in America offer an alternative view of
history. This is now backed by archeological
evidence. One wonders why, on arrival in the
Americas, the Vikings did not move south to warmer
climes. Perhaps the inhabitants of chilly Canada and
northern New England could enlighten us?

\*\*\*

The 8<sup>th</sup> Century Saga of Ragnar Lothbrok (Loðbrók means shaggy breeches), tells of his legendary raid on Lindisfarne in 793. The defenseless monks were mostly slaughtered and the rest enslaved. Their Christian god was considered weak for allowing these raids, and his son's crucifixion. Ragnar made other assaults in England and on Paris. The saga has been adapted as the basis for a successful TV series. This has further revived interest in these relentless raiders.

Today, there are Viking societies in many countries including the USA. The US also hosts a Viking biker gang and a football team. It is unlikely that they chose their names in a desire for gentility from their members and fans.

Enthused by exciting historical novels and such TV programs, many a desk-bound modern male dreams of his alter-ego slaughtering enemies and making free with admiring and willing women. Such fantasies are kept as dark secrets in our politically correct era, especially in the light of the "me too" movement. Also in this age of liberated women, some girls fantasize of themselves as shield-maidens, slaying men with abandon and standing firm in the line of battle on an equal footing.

\*\*\*

In our modern era, Christianity is in retreat in Europe. At last, Scandinavian, Scots, Irish and even English historians are re-examining the history of the Norse. Excavations in many lands have led to a revision of past inaccuracies. The excellent Jorvik Museum in the former Viking capital of northern England, now called York, depicts how civilized the Vikings became; trading, farming and much else…when there was nothing more exciting afoot that weekend.

Raiding and war were only a part of a complex civilization. Its influence reached through the rivers of Europe and via the seas as far as what is now Italy and Turkey. To this day the Russians, "the Rus" (red), are named for their Swedish ancestors, due to their dominant hair color. Even the word slave derives from the Slavs they captured on their way through central Europe as they rowed their captives to the flesh markets of the Orient.

# PROLOGUE

This novel draws heavily on the famous 21$^{st}$ Century "Saga of Blood-Axe." Discussions about the saga, recitals in thirty-eight languages and academic commentaries, have spread across social media for a few years now. If anything, its popularity is increasing.

The Saga of Blood-Axe sings the praises of a modern Viking, whose heroic deeds have become internationally renowned. We understand a film is in the offing to follow the US documentary drama series, banned in Britain, but which has attracted record audiences elsewhere. This has become the most widely pirated TV show of all time. Even the Chinese Government has failed to suppress it. A rewritten, approved version, with Blood-Axe as a Han-Chinese hero, is topping the viewing charts in Beijing. The current North Korean leader is an avid fan of the US version. It is rumored that the one thing he and the US President Trump had in common (well maybe not the only thing), was a penchant for dressing up as Vikings in the privacy of their gilded bedrooms.

If you can find no references to the Saga of Blood-Axe in your online searches, this is due to a further bout of hacking by the clandestine services of many nations. They are determined to eradicate rebellious and subversive elements in society and suppress all self-expression and freedom.

As with the earlier sagas, the author, or authors, of The Blood-Axe Saga are lost to us. In this case, they are not lost in time, but through the ability of such, so-called terrorists and their propagandists to hide in the secret labyrinths of the Dark Web.

We do know that the saga was financed by a massive response to a crowd-funding appeal using Bitcoins. Some critics claim that an Asian dictator and several rich Middle Eastern potentates were enthusiastic and substantial donors, as were thousands of donations from people like you.

***

In writing this book, closely based on the original saga, Chris Clarke interviewed hundreds of those who participated in the actual events. Chris remains in hiding. He has survived several assassination attempts.

He hopes you enjoy his book and will recommend it to others. Then, he can become stinking rich and afford visits to the Kardashians' plastic surgeons. He is intent on becoming a strikingly beautiful shield-maiden.

Bradley/Chelsea Manning is his inspiration, though he hopes for better results than either he or the Kardashians achieved.

# KEY LOCATIONS

Most of the action in the *Blood-Axe Saga* is set on a North-South axis in England, between London and York.

**Birmingham** is England's second largest city, halfway between London and York. It has a significant Muslim minority and has suffered unfortunate racial tensions, which are mentioned in this book.

**Buckinghamshire** is the name of the English county containing many of the following locations and the area where most of the action occurs.

**Newport Pagnell, Buckinghamshire** is a large village, sixty miles due north of London. It abuts one of the meanders of the River Great Ouse. This slow-flowing river then wends its muddy way onwards to the east coast. It provided a perfect entry point to the heart of England for the Vikings who sailed across the North Sea from Scandinavia.

**Little Linford** is a mixed agricultural and wooded area, close to Newport Pagnell.

**Milton Keynes, Buckinghamshire** is a large modern

city, a ten-minute drive from Newport Pagnell.

**Cranfield** is a smaller village nearby. It is now known for its high-tech University, small airfield and technology park.

**Olney** is a pretty, honey-stone village on another meander of the river Great Ouse. It is a few miles northeast of Newport Pagnell. Its old-world charm makes it a popular tourist destination.

**Hemel Hempstead** is a town between Newport Pagnell and London.

**York, the Viking Jorvik** was a walled Roman city. Later, its ready-made defensive walls led the Vikings to make it their capital. It is 158 miles north of Newport Pagnell and is situated on the River Ouse, not to be confused with the Great Ouse, further south. English rivers must be prone to oozing.

**Jokelfjord** lies across the North Sea from the UK and is one of the most northern and remote locations in Norway's Arctic Circle. It has the only glacier in Northern Europe that calves into the sea.

# CHAPTER 1

## HIS MAJESTY'S PRISON BELMARSH, SOUTH EAST LONDON, ENGLAND-2022

*"I never saw a man who looked*

*With such a wistful eye*

*Upon that little tent of blue*

*Which prisoners call the sky,*

*And every drifting cloud that went,*

*With sails of silver by."*

Oscar Wilde - The Ballad of Reading Jail

P risoner 683947, Sir Christopher Walls, looked glumly around his Spartan segregation cell. *What an awful way to end my long and successful life.* Sixty years old and balding, Chris had been a star consultant with a prestigious international firm. Then he was the gruff chief executive for a European logistics company based in Rotterdam. He had managed assets in the billions and over 60,000 employees in forty-two countries. Finally, he had turned around a moribund Dutch business school, bringing it back into the top rank of European educational institutions.

Here he was in the High Security unit of the prison, stripped of all his success. There was little for him to see in this cramped confinement. Designed to prevent suicide or other mischief, his cell was ten feet by six feet of white-painted concrete. The narrow cement bed melded seamlessly into the floor. On it laid a thin foam mattress with a cream plastic covering. Some prison bedding and a lumpy pillow were in a neat pile at one end of the bed. A stainless-steel unit was built into one corner. This combined a seat-less toilet with an integral washbasin. The room smelt of unpleasant cleaning fluids. An armored monster of a door had a viewing slit and a feeding hatch that could only be opened from the outside. There were no accessible hinges. The thin, mesh-covered window opposite the door was like an arrow slit in a medieval castle. It looked out onto a dull grey wall.

Chris Walls despaired, *There's no way I could get out of here without a small army. Even if I escaped the cell, we passed fifteen armored security gates on the way to this wing and four more within it. No gate opens without the next one being closed. The staff gain access using fingerprint touch pads. There's a facial recognition scan too. My life's over, except for frustration, tedium and mental suffering.*

Miserably, he slumped on the bed, shoulders hunched. He was dressed in his startling green and bilious yellow-patched "escape" suit. Prisoners wore these so as to be conspicuous, should they miraculously break free. *What a joke!* This could never happen at Belmarsh. It was considered the highest security prison in the UK, a place to confine terrorists and the most dangerous of murderers.

Chris reflected on this new humiliation of solitary

confinement. His external popularity had soared since his trial. His mail included proposals of marriage, complete with provocative pictures of voluptuous blondes from Russia, Poland, Scandinavia and even further afield. *Now my divorce is complete, I might take one or two up on approval, if only I could ever get out of here.* Then he remembered his true love, hopelessly waiting for him outside. His eyes welled with tears.

A week earlier, there were massed demonstrations and riots by his frenzied devotees on his behalf outside the Old Bailey court house. They resulted in Belmarsh's maximum security regime being slightly relaxed. Those of his Viking warriors who were imprisoned with him now mixed freely with the Jihadist terrorists during association periods. Still, no more than four prisoners were allowed together at one time.

Chris recalled the Governor's words.

"Right then Walls; let's hope a dose of interminable preaching of the Koran by these fanatics will calm your people down."

Chris had remained sullenly silent, casting the self-important Governor a withering look. *You silly little man.* His critical eye had seen multiple ways the inefficient prison regime could be made more cost-effective. *Once you've been a business leader, you always seek improvement.*

Now here he was in this isolation cell. To the great surprise of his jailors, his Vikings had converted the Islamists to the old Norse gods. Largely, this was through beating them into submission. The Former Jihadists changed their names to reflect their new Viking values. These included: Asger, (spear of a god); Balder, (bearer of light); Bjarke, (bear); Gosta, (staff of a god); Ivar, (bowman) and many more. Their beards remained. Prisoner Wall's tougher confinement resulted from the related riots.

*The guards here are ignoramuses. They dehumanize every aspect of my life.* He especially hated the intimate daily searches for weapons or other contraband as material. *As if I could get my hands on anything in here.*

"Stand up Prisoner Walls. Get'cha clothes off. Lean forward and spread 'em."

Initially, he'd given them a mouthful in his broad Liverpool accent,

"Touch me pal and mi men'll cut yer balls off."

Then he restrained himself, remembering how the prison riot squad had Tasered him during an earlier outburst. *They've always got the squad on call, so best not push them too far. They get bored and love to take it out on us.* His tormentors also suppressed their anger and desire to rough him up. He was now over sixty and famous. If he had a heart attack, they would cop it. Also, a fellow guard was recently beheaded in his own home and under strange circumstances. It made them think.

"All right grandad, you're all clear. Here's the book you ordered from the National Library."

Grumpily, Chris dressed. Opening the leather-bound volume, he began to read the first paragraph. It transported him back over a thousand years.

"Gísla saga Súrssona Kafli Þaðerupphaf á ofanverðumhansdögum. Þorkellhétmaður; hannvarkallaðurskerauki; hannbjó í Súrnadalogvarhersiraðnafnbót. Hann áttisérkonu er Ísgerðurhétogsonuþrjábarna; héteinn Ari, annarGísli, þriðjiÞorbjörn, hannvarþeirrayngstur, oguxuallirupppheimaþar."

It had taken him a while to master the old Icelandic Norse despite his education in modern languages at Liverpool University. Now, he savored every poetic phrase of *Gisla Saga*. It told of a young warrior who was honor-bound to kill a brother-in-law. This was to avenge a second relative. The hero was hunted down and slaughtered, but to his everlasting fame.

Feeling sorry for himself, Chris Walls put the book down, transported back into his Viking fantasy. *I need to die in battle with a sword in my hand, to be remembered forever and to feast in Valhalla with the gods. What did I do wrong to end my days trapped in this dump?*

\*\*\*

In the Prison Governor's Office, Detective Chief Superintendent Masher of New Scotland Yard's anti-terrorist group was engaged in a flaming row with the Governor. Masher was a bulky man, formerly muscular, but largely gone to fat. His suit seemed to strain at its stitching. A bullet head merged seamlessly with his shoulders. His arms looked as though they would burst from his sleeves at any moment. He had a flattened broken nose. It had developed a boozer's red and purple veins at its bulbous end. His menacing eyes, hung with dark bags, were always slightly bloodshot. Now, he leaned over the Governor's desk and roared into his face. He was practically frothing at the mouth. His cheeks glowed bright red, his eyes blazing.

"You must have been freaekin' crazy to allow these two groups to mix! They were bad enough on their own. Now we have twice the problem. We could both lose our jobs over this."

"Don't worry. It's all calm in here now."

"Don't worry, is it? The Islamists and Vikings are fighting each other on city streets around the country. It's Jihadists against Vikings and apostates. Take a look."

He grabbed a black remote control from the desk and clicked on the BBC's live coverage.

The center of Birmingham, a city in the center of England, was ablaze. There were burning shops and cars. As the camera zoomed out from a distance, a pall of choking smoke hung over the buildings. An excited reporter was commenting from a helicopter. His words were rapid and garbled.

"You can see the dense cloud of ash rising to 20,000 feet. Air traffic is totally disrupted."

The Governor gasped. Another newsman near Birmingham city center was wearing a blue BBC flack-jacket and Kevlar helmet. His accompanying cameraman was filming a police riot squad being forced back under a hail of axes, spears and Molotov cocktails, behind their Perspex shields. A smoking white phosphorous grenade tumbled high over the police lines. Their shield-wall broke. They sprinted for their lives. White phosphorus particles burned through shields, uniforms, flesh and bone of the slow or unfortunate. They were the quick and the dead.

A dozen of their comrades were left screaming, writhing in agony as the frenzied mob closed around them through the smoke. Shots rang out. The intrepid reporter ducked. He shouted into his microphone above the noises of conflict.

"It appears that both factions have started shooting at the police…"

There was a loud crack. The camera wobbled briefly, showing the interviewer's body splayed out on the road. There was a neat bullet hole in his forehead. Blood pooled around him. A burst of gunfire and an explosion followed. The camera wavered again and fell. The screen went blank.

# CHAPTER 2

## LITTLE LINFORD GOLF COURSE
## THREE YEARS EARLIER

*"Golf is a good walk spoiled"*

Mark Twain

Three years earlier, Chris Walls' bald head was sweating with tension. He glowered as he took what should have been his last putt on the 18th hole. Three other old men variously smirked, shrugged or looked up at the sky as he missed the easiest of shots from six feet. Chris was a notoriously bad golfer, but ever keen to improve. Flustered by his ineptitude, he took two more putts to finish. As usual, he and his partner lost. Handicaps never seemed to work in favor of Chris.

After the game, they settled down to the serious part of the day; gin and tonics in the clubhouse. Lizzie, the barmaid smiled indulgently at them over her ample bosom as she polished some pint glasses. There they were, three grumpy grandads in their usual corner, ill-temperedly setting the world's problems to rights.

John Chandler was a local gentleman farmer and recently retired Investment Banker. Stick thin, he was six-foot-three and bore a scar on his cheek from an Afghan bullet. He had served with the Grenadier Guards in Helmand province. Educated at Harrow and Oxford, he was holding forth in his upper-class braying voice.

"What Britain needs is more backbone. No one takes risks any more. The nanny state feather-beds everyone. There's no need to work hard or even at all. Kids can sit at home playing video games or go to university forever. Half the population is working for the state, overpaid and with no penalties for cock-ups. I get so frustrated. In our day, we could have done something about it. Now it's too late. No one listens to us."

The others nodded in sad agreement. Chris hated retirement. He felt the same way John did. Since he retired from his last job leading the Dutch business school, he felt his successors had let it slide. The institution was no longer ranked number one in the Netherlands. *My life has been just an elaborate charade, signifying nothing.* As John spoke, he gazed sadly into his gin. Looking up, he responded,

"Well John, at least we can enjoy fresh air and share a game and a drink here twice a week. My wife's glad to get me out of the house."

Chris's wife, Drika, was a strong-minded woman. A full head taller than he and built like a Dutch cart-horse; she kept him in line. With pursed lips, she read all his emails, deleting the jokes whilst muttering,

"No smut."

If Chris drank too much, she nagged him endlessly. He was forced to accompany her on long walks for exercise.

She kept Chris on the straight and narrow. Some said she ruled the house with a rod of iron. She encouraged his golf, telling her friends,

"It'sa means of keeping him out of trouble."

\*\*\*

The majority of homes in the English villages around Chris's home in northeast Buckinghamshire and its neighboring county of Bedfordshire were built from the local, golden sandstone. Many were thatched cottages. This added to their charm, essential for competing in the annual Best Kept Village award. The contest entailed flower baskets overflowing with colorful blooms hanging from every lamp-post, immaculately clean sidewalks and a profusion of twee little emporia.

There were many tea rooms and cake shops. Cramped sales space sold knickknacks and clichéd mottos on wooden plaques or fridge magnets. Chris especially loathed these. The tiny pottery foxes, tea-mugs saying Best Grandad, signs reading, The Kitchen is the Heart of the Home, and flowered table mats drove him apoplectic. As Drika spent ages examining some tasteless kitsch, he day-dreamed, *I'd love to sweep armfuls of bric-a-brac onto the floor, in broken heaps. These smug little villages need a good shaking up.*

More to the needs of his stomach were the traditional butchers. They hung hares and un-plucked pheasants in their windows. Delicatessens sold country pâtés, jams, veal and ham pies, and chutneys. He loved the village pubs with oak-beamed ceilings, traditional ales, hearty steak, Guinness and oyster pies. There were bustling farmers' markets in the village squares once a week.

\*\*\*

Mike Jackson, blue-eyed, blond-haired and mustachioed was one of Chris's long-suffering golfing partners. A retired air vice-Marshal and a fighter pilot during the Second World War, he was happy living in the past. He dreamed of his days intercepting Soviet bombers in his Mach 2 Eurofighter high over the North Sea. The acceleration from the steep afterburner takeoff was like a kick in the back of his seat. His small stature was irrelevant when he had 30,000 pounds of thrust powering him forward and upward. His finger was always itching over the red trigger guard for his rotary cannon and missiles. To his frustration, these encounters invariably ended with the Russians turning away with cheeky waves from their crews. How he would have liked to have blasted them into oblivion.

Nowadays, Mike took a great interest in local history. There was plenty of it. The surrounding rich, rolling farmland was scattered with old manor houses. It had been fought over in the Wars of the Roses. Gayhurst House, just up the road, had been a center for the Gunpowder Plotters. They tried to blow up King James 1st, of England, and his Parliament early in the 17th Century.

During the English Civil War of the 1640s the area formed a no-man's-land between the Cavaliers of King Charles' 1st Cavaliers and Oliver Cromwell's roundheads. Nearby Bletchley Park was the Enigma, code-breaking headquarters in World War II. They decoded Hitler's most secret battle plans. Mike loved history, with all its tales of derring-do.

He was particularly pleased to attend a historical reenactment at the site of an English Civil war fortification in nearby Newport Pagnell.

\*\*\*

On the occasion of a reenactment of the battle of Newport Pagnell of 1643, a relatively minor skirmish in the English Civil War, John Chandler was throwing a Champagne party. He had assembled his golfing partners, family, ex-clients and friends in a big tent on his lawn adjoining the river Great Ouse.

Chris Walls enthusiastically waved a half-eaten ham sandwich at John, gripping his third pint of strong amber ale in the other hand. Drika was engaged in gossip with her friends and had missed him surreptitiously refilling his glass.

"John, that was a wonderful event. The banners, the cannon fire, the Royalists and Roundheads brandishing swords and thrusting pikes at each other. It was fun to see the camp followers preparing the meals before the battle and helping the wounded later. Those were the days."

Mike Jackson joined in. His eyes glowed with enthusiasm. The other golfers gathered around.

"They certainly were Chris. No nanny state then. No young MBAs trying to run things."

Ever-combative, Chris leapt to the defense of MBAs.

"Wait a minute John. Those from my Dutch school all had real experience before we fine-tuned them. Many went on to run important global businesses with great success."

Towering above him, John Chandler placed a placatory hand on Chris's arm. Chris wrinkled his brow with worry, lest he spill the excellent beer.

"Yes! Yes, Chris. Mike's only saying that life's pretty boring these days, especially for us. Imagine what it was like to be a leader of Royalist cavalry, charging through the ripening crops and sabering Parliamentary infantry as they fled the bloody field."

Chris looked concerned at the thought. *Riding horses was never my idea of fun. Besides, the Cromwellian cavalry were known as the Ironsides. They seemed to do most of the slaughtering. Being a Cavalier was to be hunted, imprisoned or worse. I've seen the breastplates from that time in museums. Some bore ragged half-inch holes torn by musket balls. One or two had been twisted and ripped asunder by round shots from cannon.*

Despite his initial reaction, Chris retired to bed that evening gaining mildly drunken enthusiasm for the idea. Drika, whom he met when she was a lecturer at his business school, had taken charge of his life then, and did so now. As often happened when he had imbibed too much, she made him sleep on the couch. Its wooden arm gave him a crick in the neck. Still, his vivid and colorful dreams were full of adrenaline and military glory. Naturally, Chris was a general, directing the ebb and flow of battle. He saw flashing blades, Cavalier hats with feathers streaming in the wind, as his troops pursued fleeing Roundheads and cut them down.

\*\*\*

To escape the drudgery of retirement, Chris too took to reading more about local events from bygone times. He delved deeply into the Saxon period of the 9th Century. It emerged that the river Great Ouse, which ran through the village of Newport Pagnell and on to Olney, a nearby market town, was an important ancient frontier. The Danes had sailed their shallow-draft long-ships as far as here to ravage the countryside. A tenuous and short-lived peace was agreed by King Alfred the Great.

To the north of the river, the Dane-Law applied. There, the Vikings ruled from distant York, which they called Jorvik. South of the river, the country was held by the Saxons. They ruled from Winchester, west and south of London, through a network of noble earls and thegns.

The more Chris studied, the more he grew to admire the Vikings. *These were my kind of people. They didn't suffer fools gladly. Indeed, fools suffered rather badly. My ancestors were from Ireland. I must have Norse blood in me. Hell, I'm practically a Viking.* Resting his head on his chin, he gazed dreamily across the fields beyond Drika's rose garden. There, he envisioned well-run villages, where weary warriors went to rest between adventures and battles. Yes, he could see it all. The thought of captive slave-girls toiling in the fields and kitchens added spice to his reverie.

That night he enjoyed a stiff Malt whiskey as he read some more by a warm log fire. In his sleep, an idea began to form.

\*\*\*

In front of a bigger blazing log hearth in the golf club, many foursomes were drying off. It was pouring down on the course. Flashes of lightning led them to abandon their games. Chris felt that the frequent claps of thunder and flickering bright light provided an excellent backdrop for him to expound his vision. Their drama added to his natural charisma, as he enthusiastically described his notion.

"Look, we need to do something. Here we are, wasting away our last years. What've we got to look forward to? There are reunion dinners where the young whippersnappers tolerate us old fossils and the pretty young girls ignore us. There are rare invitations to Buckingham Palace Garden Parties. They allow our wives to preen themselves and boast to their friends, and for what? We queue for hours for cucumber sandwiches without ever meeting the King. He's nearly dead anyway."

One or two were shocked at this last remark. A member in a wheel chair pushed himself into the circle to listen. Another, troubled with his prostate, desperately suppressed his urge to visit the men's room, so he could hear Chris's ideas.

"Many of us enjoyed the reenactment of the Battle of Newport Pagnell last month; entertained by good old John Chandler and encouraged by Mike Jackson here. I've started boning up on the history of the area. It turns out that in Viking times, Newport Pagnell was a frontier town—with all that that implies. There were raids, invasions, battles and all the rest. The Vikings made the English Civil War lot look like a bunch of sissies. Their battlefield was everything that they could reach from the wild, wide ocean, from rivers and on horseback."

The crowd grew and shuffled closer. Many had enjoyed recent TV shows about the Vikings. Chris's excitement seemed to electrify his audience. What was he going to propose?

# CHAPTER 3

## IN JOHN CHANDLER'S CONVERTED BARN, SOME MONTHS LATER

*"The King, Volsung, had a noble hall constructed, so that a huge Oak tree stood inside it. Its limbs blossomed fair above the roof... Therein did men feast, drink and hear wonderful tales."*

From the Volsunga Saga

The recently formed Great Ouse Villages Viking Appreciation Society (GOVVAS), met in its Great Mead Hall. Making suitable changes to the old wooden barn in a remote part of John Chandler's estate was easy. Local carpenters, stonemasons and other physical types liked the Viking idea too and gave freely of their labor and muscle.

Half the municipal planning committee were members, so the town council swiftly rubber-stamped permission for the barn conversion. An adjoining footpath was diverted. The inevitable objections from walkers and country busybodies were quashed with the aid of a little persuasion from nocturnal visits by masked assailants with shotguns from the Young Farmers Club. Prying eyes were discouraged. There was something a little embarrassing about grown men playing at being Vikings, fun though it was.

The Hall was truly magnificent with old wooden beams

and a king-post, trussed roof. They built a large open hearth to keep the huge space warm and to roast animal carcasses. After an asthmatic member was hospitalized with carbon monoxide poisoning and everyone's eyes streamed from the smoke, a proper stone chimney was added, though not strictly in period.

Because bear, stag and other heads to decorate the walls were difficult to obtain, due to animal rights legislation and import restrictions, a member's plastic factory turned out realistic substitutes. The council of members rejected a suggestion that the eyes would light up, as demeaning the dignity of the place. Chris placated the disgruntled advocates of electric eyes.

"After a few horns of strong ale, you'll see the eyes light up anyway."

The plastic factory molded great round shields bearing Viking symbols, axes and spears to lend further realism to the décor. Hung around the walls in the flickering dimness of the torchlight, they looked totally authentic.

Great trestle tables and benches were constructed for feasting. There were no issues with the menus. Pigs were plentiful in local farms. John Chandler kept corralled wild boar in a large enclosure. The woodlands abounded with game-birds and Muntjac deer. Decades earlier, some of these snaggle-toothed animals from China escaped from the nearby Duke of Bedford's estate. They had spread throughout the UK.

There remained one intractable problem. It was discussed in the Viking Council. Chris, who had adopted the Viking sobriquet of Jarl Chris, (meaning the rank of Earl), took the lead.

"Look we have to be practical. We've tried brewing beer from old Norse recipes and I'm sorry, but it's crap. Most of us can't stand mead. I need whiskey. Surely the Vikings would have traded or stolen that from our Celtic cousins?"

Sysselman (meaning head of internal affairs, policeman and administrator), tall John Chandler with his scarred cheek, was a stickler for historical accuracy. So was diminutive and blond-haired Mike Jackson. He was now leader of the Jarl's personal warriors, the House-Karls. Chandler asked,

"Do we want to be Vikings or lily-livered wannabes?"

Jarl Chris was fixated on getting his next whiskey. He thought, *The way to carry the meeting is to keep the mead for special occasions and get some decent ale.* As was his wont, he used his reputation for having a short fuse to face down the much taller John Chandler. He worked himself into such a fake fury that a vein in his brow pulsed with rage and he hurled himself towards John.

"Who're you calling lily-livered pal. Last man who did that's still in orbit."

He allowed himself to be restrained by a couple of burley young farmers as John blanched and took a few hasty steps backwards. In his brief time as an officer in the guards, John had fought tough Afghanis from a distance, but the volatile and bellicose Chris terrified him. Oiks from rough Liverpool backgrounds had a frightening reputation. Chris switched to a more emollient tone.

"Look we could hide the barrels of real ale behind the serving tables at the back of the hall. The whiskey could be decanted into mead containers, as long as we don't mix them up. We've a consignment of drinking horns on its way from Norway. No one need know the difference."

There was banging of approving fists on the tables. The mead and beer mugs bounced. A mug fell onto the rushes on the floor. One of John Chandler's massive and shaggy Irish Wolfhounds bounded for it and licked up the beer. Chris gave the dog an approving look.

"Nice dogs those, John. Now that's decided let's move on to the next agenda item. Sigurd here (formerly Ben), wants to be allowed to take part in the reenactments. We've seen how his electric wheelchair can get him about. He wants to add scythes to the wheels like a form of chariot."

The debate around this became quite heated. Sigurd had many friends in the group. Others felt sorry for him. Eventually, a compromise was reached. In the reenactments, he would carry a bow and arrows, seated in an ox cart, as personal escort to the Jarl. Both honor and authenticity were satisfied.

They discussed other matters. They agreed that suitable buxom serving wenches were to be recruited. The vote on this was unanimous. Also, given the geriatric nature of many in the club, they agreed to recruit some of the local fire brigade and farm laborers to form the famous Viking shield-walls. Plentiful Porta-loos were to be acquired for the many with prostate problems.

Shield-walls were formidable tactical barriers against attackers. The interlocked shields of the front rank stopped enemy charges dead. The Vikings stabbed spears and long swords in between and under their shields. Those with axes crushed helmets and skulls with swinging blows over the top of the wall. Axes could also be used to hook down the shields opposite. If there were incoming arrows or hurled spears, the second rank lifted their shields over the heads of those in front to protect them. It was a brutally efficient method of slaughter. As the wall advanced in steady steps over fallen enemies, wounded foemen were trampled and killed by the following ranks.

\*\*\*

The local smithy's bellows worked day and night as the metal workers abandoned their modern manufacture of horseshoes and decorative wrought iron gates to make dozens of suitable axe, arrow and spear heads. They hammered the glowing metal into long and short swords, helmets and the bosses for the round wooden shields.

The local smith was given the name Solveig, (this means from the House of Strength). He was a blond-haired giant with a lantern jaw and fearsome temper. He recruited fellow smiths from around the county to assist him. The glistening muscles of his men bulged with each hammer blow. Molten iron lit the room with a hellish glow as it was poured into the molds for axes. He yelled above the hammering on anvils and the hissing of quenching metal blades.

"Come on lads, we need 1,000 sets of kit to put on a great show next week."

\*\*\*

A year later, the scene at Buckingham Palace was very orderly. The doddery old King looked especially frail, even compared to his last TV appearance. An equerry whispered the names in his ear as he invested each of the many to be honored. They waited in line in traditional morning suits, comprising grey-striped trousers and long-tailed black jackets.

Jarl Chris fulminated, awaiting his turn. *I should've received a gong before, if that damned civil servant of David Cameron's hadn't been so upset. I called him a dunderhead during the European leadership training at our business school. He was a dunderhead, too. Still, Drika looks well pleased. She'll be Lady Drika in a few minutes. She'll love to put on even more airs and graces. She'll become impossible. She tries to manage everything I do as it is.*

One of the wilder Royal Princes had attended a Viking re-enactment and arranged for Chris's name to go forward for a knighthood. The Prince had loved the feast in the Mead Hall and had scored with a shapely local wench in a dark corner. He was assured that his wife would never know. What happened in the Mead Hall stayed in the Mead Hall. Cell phones and cameras were banned. Anyway, everyone was so drunk that they fell among the rushes with the dogs in the smoky darkness, girly legs thrown over many of them.

On an earlier occasion, an intrepid member of the tabloid press had somehow bluffed his way in. A throwing axe had smashed his camera in two, right out of his hands. He spent the night tied naked to a table while some of the local girls made free with his person and took their own blackmail pictures with their own sneaked-in cell phones.

\*\*\*

That evening, Jarl and now Sir Christopher Walls, dined with his family and friends at the Savoy Hotel in London before being driven home from his investiture in a hired limousine. He always arranged his family dos there. His daughter's wedding reception had cost him a small fortune.

Chris had retired comfortably off. Now he and his warriors were making a fortune. Without intention, they had created a substantial business.

\*\*\*

In a huge field near the former Viking capital of York, tourists and locals were queueing to buy their tickets to the Viking reenactment. They parked their cars for five pounds for the day in another field. Eight thrall couples in costume (the lowest rank in Viking society and virtually slaves) were struggling to keep up with the payments.

"That'll be fifteen pounds for the three of you Sir. A program is fifty pence. T-shirts, Thor's hammers on neck chains, helmets and swords for the kids are all on sale at the stalls."

Around the field where battle was to commence, the St. John's Ambulance teams gave first aid to anyone who needed it. Their vehicles stood by ready to rush anyone injured or suffering a heart attack off to hospital.

Outside the Viking tents, womenfolk served up hearty stews to visitors. Others braided hair for some of the children.

Solveig, the smith, and his team, reluctantly checked the rubber or plastic guards on the edges of every weapon. The Jarl was most insistent that safety was a priority. Elsewhere, Vikings took their frustrations out with sharpened axes, hurling them at wooden targets to entertain the visitors. The crowd clapped when the force of one impact split the target in two.

Some of the more sporting policemen shed their helmets for silly Viking ones with horns. They would make the evening papers. The Chief Constable saw it as good public relations for the Yorkshire force.

Jarl Sir Chris smiled as he regarded the area set aside for the Anglo-Saxon camp.

"You know fellas; it amazes me that people want to be Saxons and to lose so often."

John Chandler, the lanky and scar faced ex-guardsman

chortled,

"Maybe it's like being the US at Soccer. They mostly lose, but at least the women play well. As to the Saxons, we do let 'em win every now and then, when the history permits."

Jarl Chris beamed.

"And remember that fat fellow, who plays the Christian Bishop. The crowd loves it when he trips over his robes and his miter falls off as he runs away. Even better if the Vikings chop him down. Maybe the Saxons are all Christians?"

John gloated at all he saw.

"Look Chris, there must be 5,000 people in here already and more to come. Even after paying for the police presence and the hire of the fields we'll make a fortune.

"And this is the fifth event so far this year. With the fifty pounds annual membership fees we now charge and the money from events in the Mead Hall, we are on the way to making millions. I've just set up franchising agreements for the US, Canada, and even Norway. Our Cayman Island company is sheltering most of it from taxes."

Mike Jackson, the diminutive ex-fighter pilot with the blond hair and moustache, chipped in.

"That's great and as we three own it all between us, we have more money than we'll ever need, even for our grandchildren. One thing bothers me. The bigger this gets the more we stray from historical accuracy. Those plastic helmets with horns for the kids are an example."

John Chandler patted him on the shoulder. They made an odd pair, the lanky and the tiny. He tried to placate Mike.

"Well we keep the reenactments strictly to historic rectitude. No horned helmets on the battlefield. Those kids' helmets are a top seller. We clear a pound profit on each one. They usually want swords and shields too. Our Chinese suppliers will be making a new range for the autumn."

Mike remained unmollified,

"I know we have three million pounds set aside for the planned Viking museum in Milton Keynes and a government grant for another million, but someone will ask questions eventually."

Jarl Sir Chris was not interested in sales of Viking Jam, Viking Mead or Blood-Axe brand ale. The latter was now a popular guest beer in many pubs nationwide, complete with the fierce Viking-head logo on the beer pumps. Larger supermarkets were carrying it in bottles.

\*\*\*

 In their tent, after the Yorkshire reenactment, John Chandler and Jarl Chris Walls were interviewing candidates to join the Vikings. There was quite a queue outside.

John and Chris were questioning a bearded and tattooed man already wearing a Viking costume. He seemed tense and sat very erect. John liked his soldierly bearing. He was answering well.

"I've been a member of a Viking society in Poland for some years, but I live near London. Your organization seems better than ours."

Jarl Chris asked him why he had joined the Polish group.

"I became a French foreign legionnaire at 21 and was with them for five years. I missed the action and sense of camaraderie after that. I guess I was lonely and depressed. I turned to alcohol. Then I saw a movie about the Vikings. That was the life! I did some research and found the Poles."

John Chandler gave him a penetrating look. He wanted to check him out further.

"Why did you join the Legion?"

"Two reasons Sir. I was being hunted by the police, after glassing a man's face in a pub fight. He started it, Sir. The adventure was attractive too."

"Which regiment of the Legion were you in?"

The man proudly puffed out his chest.

"Deuxième régiment de parachutistes étrangers, Sir."

"Ah! The best, the paras."

Jarl Chris loved to show off his language skills, especially in French. He asked various questions, but was disappointed. The oaf speaks only legionnaire's slang. Would he make a good Viking though? Do we want criminal types? After the potential recruit left the tent, Jarl Chris, turned to John Chandler.

"His French is from the gutter. Can you control animals like him?"

"What sort do you think we get in the British Army. He's exactly what I was used to. He'll slot right in."

The Jarl smiled.

"Oh well, it's great that we can provide a sort of social service by keeping thugs like him off the street and channeling his energy into mock battles. I suppose that sociopaths have to become criminals, soldiers or policemen."

***

Chris was bored with the photographs that he was asked to sign and even with his personal fan club. He kept that well away from his wife. Drika would definitely not approve of the erotic suggestions proposed by some of his more callipygous fans. Their photographs did stir him though. *I don't want all this publicity. Mmm, maybe I would like to get to know just a few of the fans.* He quashed the next discussion about what a great business they now had.

"Look I've spent years running much larger businesses than this. I want more than us offering long-ship rides up the River Thames. Besides, I can't go out these days without the paparazzi or people bothering me for autographs. Mike can handle the TV series and the history stuff. He likes that. You, John, are still a wheeler-dealer Investment Banker. You like the money side. I need something more. I can't think what, but there must be something."

# CHAPTER 4

## THE ARRIVAL OF THE SEER

*"You must never sacrifice your sons or daughters by burning them alive, practice black magic, be a fortuneteller, witch or sorcerer, caste spells, ask ghosts or spirits for help or consult the dead"*

Deuteronomy 18:10-12

Jarl Sir Chris was playing a round of golf with three of his Vikings. He and his partner were well behind. His bald pate sweated with concentration and stress. His game never seemed to improve. In the clouds overhead, thunderheads loomed ominously dark.

House Karl Sigurd, a muscle-bound opponent with a bull neck and close-cropped head, enjoyed winding Chris up, which was always very easy. He teased Chris now.

"Time to pray to those Nordic gods now Jarl. Even they can't help you."

Chris looked up at the threatening weather. *Maybe, just maybe, rain might stop play. I think I'll try a little wind-up of my own.* He made sure they all saw him touch the Thor's hammer talisman which hung round his neck on a silver chain. Theatrically, he spread his arms wide, palms up to the sky. In a booming voice, he invoked the god.

"Oh, mighty Thor, punish this unbeliever. Show him thy power!"

Pretending to ignore this, Sigurd moved forward. He began the upward swing to take his shot. He merely glanced back over his shoulder at Chris in sneering disbelief. Flash! Bang! Lightning shot through the up-swung club. It felled the whole group to the ground. As the others struggled to their feet, they saw the blackened, crispy, dead hands of Sigurd fused to the twisted metal of the club. It had conducted the massive current through his body.

The other three stood shocked and open-mouthed. Stilling his own trembling hands and in best laconic Sean Connery style, Chris casually remarked,

"Well I shuppose we'll just have to abandon the game then."

\*\*\*

For some months before that fateful golf game, one of the concession stalls at the Viking reenactments was doing a roaring trade. Ever looking for a deal, John Chandler proposed a board motion to buy the female owner out.

"She has marketable ideas to franchise. With our

company's greater volume and buying power, we could make a killing. Those statues and symbols of the various Norse gods and some of the fortune cookie type predictions she sells would make a wonderful international franchise. Some of the stuff is high quality. I have a full-sized figure of Odin's black Raven at home. My wife hates the thing, which is the main reason I insist on keeping it in the house. Ha! If the grand kids misbehave, I tell the little blighters it'll come and peck their eyes out when they're asleep. If we cut the quality of her stuff just a little, there would be higher margins."

Grumpy as ever, Chris took umbrage at this. He waved the proposal aside before the rest of the board could respond.

"We need to invite the stall owner, Freyja, into the ownership of the company. She could really bring more excitement into what's just becoming another boring business. Hell! We all left that behind. True Vikings can do so much more. Anyway, it'd stop the feminists moaning at us."

*** 

Freyja had a striking presence; pale, tall and whipcord hard. She had riveting black eyes that delved into men's souls. Her costume and make up were like something from a vampire movie. Her hair was dyed coal-black; long and unkempt. Her sharp fingernails were painted shiny black, with a drop of glistening blood-red on each tip. Her tattooed arms bulged from a tight-fitting leather jacket. Dark lipstick and panda eyes completed the frightful picture. Despite all this, she oozed sex appeal and melted the hearts of both men and many women.

Formerly Janet Winslet-Parker, she was the only daughter of a real Earl and heir to a 400-year-old mansion in Sussex, plus a considerable fortune. As the wealthy do, her parents had dispatched her to a posh boarding school. There, of all things, she excelled in physics and electronics, building robots and computers in the school labs. Her interest was partly fueled by a crush on the petite and pretty Physics teacher. Janet took the dominant role in their affair, despite the risks to the teacher's career.

She went off the rails when she was seventeen and was expelled from the school for getting half of her class hooked on heroin. A psychologist wrote,

"She shows sociopathic tendencies. These may be the result of brain trauma. She says she was knocked unconscious in a fall from a horse at age eleven. I recommend a brain scan to investigate this further."

Her father used his friendship with the British Home Secretary to keep the police out of it. His daughter was pleased he was losing sleep over the threat to his reputation. *You never cared for me, even as a baby. Where were the hugs? You sent me off to boarding school as soon as you could get rid of me.*

Then, Janet had run off with a group of new-age travelers. She attracted serious money to their commune under her then alias of Mystic Anna. Reading Tarot cards, telling fortunes and selling herbal cures, she attracted quite a following as a white witch. There were rumors that she helped women with brutal husbands by use of certain potions that made them docile and obedient.

Her bearded hippie partner ditched her for another girl. Devastated and bitter, she abandoned the travelers and became self-sufficient. *Alone again. I'll get my revenge on men.*

She took market stalls around the country, selling new-age trinkets. She was astonished how many gullible people flocked to buy polished stones with magical properties and other nonsense. As a sideline, she built a following of aspiring white witches. They bought her books of spells and paid for courses in the arcane arts at evening classes. Left wing municipalities funded some of these, on the grounds of female empowerment and cultural diversity.

Observing the Viking reenactment in Newport Pagnell, she saw a huge commercial opportunity and the chance to dominate the males. There was also the potential fun of various steamy affairs with both the handsome would-be Vikings and the attractive women in the group. She chose the Viking name Freyja, after the goddess of love, sex, death and war. That list pretty well covered her desires.

Recognizing a good thing when she saw it, she was doing well with the Vikings. In addition, she began to weave her seductive magic around Jarl Sir Chris. He was quite cute and really gullible.

\*\*\*

In the boardroom of Viking Enterprises GOVVA plc the Finance Director tried to revive John's idea to buy out Freyja.

"Come on Chris, John has a good idea. You only like her, because she has witchy black hair, kinky tattoos and ginormous breasts."

Choosing not to be angry, Chris replied, smiling,

"Not at all. Admittedly, the boobs are a draw, but if you think my wife, Drika, would put up with any hanky-panky, you must be joking. Freyja's vital to my next idea. We have to make our Viking horde more realistic."

Mike Jackson, always keen to bring things back to the

brutal reality of the ancient Norsemen, asked,

"How?"

Chris smiled knowingly.

"All in good time Mike, you'll have to wait and see."

\*\*\*

Three weeks later it was the Spring Equinox. The northernmost woods of Norway were still deathly cold. A dusting of fresh snow lay on the trails. The nights were long, lit only by the stars and the Aurora Borealis.

Inside the rough-hewn log meeting hut, Jarl Chris and a select group of his chosen leaders huddled shivering in their borrowed wolf and bear furs. Chris had brought along his weedy nephew Joe. He was a bespectacled and prematurely balding IT geek with greasy hair, and generally held in low esteem among the gung-ho Vikings. When the others were not around, Freyja enjoyed talking electronics with him and discussing her ideas for drones, artificial intelligence and robotics.

From the front of the room, Freyja stood by a screen and solemnly lectured them on Norse mythology and the gods. Occasionally, her dark eyes flashed. Gesturing with long pointed black nails, she played the all-male audience like a harp. Her voice varied between a breathy whisper and a shrill screaming shout. It was quite a performance.

Little Mike Jackson shivered a little. It was freezing in the room and rather creepy. He noticed that Freyja never used the word mythology, even once. Though there was clearly electric power in the room, as the projector was working, Freyja insisted on turning off the heaters and using black candles as the only other source of heat and light. He stuffed his gloved hands into his pockets to prevent frostbite. Everyone's breath condensed in the chilled air. Joe wiped his misted glasses with a gloved hand.

Freyja showed illustrations of each of the gods in turn. Since the lightning strike at the golf club, most of the listeners held her in some awe.

Some said she had trained Jarl Chris in conjuring the lightning that electrocuted their colleague. Everyone knew she had been personally mentoring him before that. It even seemed that she was replacing John Chambers as number two in the Viking pecking order. She looked pointedly at Mike, who seemed not to be paying full attention.

"You already know some of this, but interrupt if you don't understand."

No one dared move a muscle, let alone break her flow. She wore no furs, just a tight black leather tunic.

Somehow, she stayed warm. Her eyes seemed to be circled in charcoal. Her cheeks sported new runic tattoos. She waved towards the screen.

"Jörmungandr is the giant serpent that circles our entire world with his tail in his mouth. When the time comes he will begin the next cycle of destruction and renewal.

As you know, this is Odin, most powerful of the gods. He is a shape-changer and can appear amongst humans at will and in any guise. He is the god of battles and war-strength. He also commands the famous Valkyries, who bear off the dead from the field of blood.

"This is his brother Loki, the trickster. He is one of my favorites. He is another shape-shifter. He can appear as any fish or any animal."

"Here we have Dellingr, the personification of dawn."

She noticed their attention flagging. Reaching into a hand-woven bag she said,

"Here take this. It will intensify our experience."

As if passing out communion, she fed each of her audience a tiny salt-spoonful of a mashed, bitter mushroomy substance. Instantly, one or two Vikings became violently sick and sweated. They began seeing the elves and giants from her screen dancing among them. Some felt they could make great leaps into the air, falling over when they tried it.

The amanita muscaria, commonly known as fly agaric, is the red-capped toadstool with white flecks of northern woodlands. Mushrooming books usually list it as poisonous. In reality, it is a powerful hallucinogenic, much used by the Sami people who herd reindeer in the Arctic Circle. The leaping reindeer of the Christmas stories really exist in Lapland. Craving the salts, the deer lick the places where Sami shamans urinate after eating the magic mushrooms. One of the effects is that objects appear to change size. To step over even the smallest twig, the deer make great jumps into the air.

\*\*\*

That night they each had vivid and sometimes frightening dreams. Next day, several of the younger men swore that Freyja had visited them in ways they would never forget. Chris's nephew, Joe, knew she had ridden him in the night but said nothing. He felt wonderful. His previously reedy voice now boomed, much to the surprise of his companions. He felt strong and, uncharacteristically, punched one man in the nose when he made fun of Joe's deep new tone.

Chris stirred in his furs. He felt a pain along in his upper arms and tried to rub it away. He opened his rheumy eyes. Mysteriously, he now sported square brown tattoos of the tree of life symbol, Yggdrasil, on both limbs. *My wife'll bloody kill me when she sees these.* Yet, somehow, he too felt infused with great power. *Maybe it's a placebo effect, or the results of that damned toadstool. All the same, I feel infused with energy and strength.*

One of the older men was missing. They searched the birch-woods outside. A cloak of newly fallen snow obscured any tracks. They fanned out amongst the trees. A large dog, a malamute, was tearing at something. Joe went to investigate, calling the others.

The partly devoured body lay naked and eviscerated. Its residual heat had melted the snow a little. Blood stained the whiteness around the corpse. Bending, Joe rolled it over. There were curious deep claw marks on its back. After some debate they delayed notifying the authorities till their training ended a few days later.

The Norwegian inquest found that their colleague had died of a heart attack and been clawed by a bear. Due to the personal intervention of an old college friend of John Chandler, high up in the British Foreign Office, the strange visiting businessmen were allowed to leave without further investigation.

\*\*\*

The day after they discovered the corpse, Freyja solemnly gathered them together for the ceremony to select names for the men and their weapons.

"Henceforth, Jarl Chris, you will bear the heroic Viking name of Blood-Axe. Your long sword will be named Skull-Splitter"

She daubed some sacred ash on his cheeks. He felt even stronger, as though he was twenty years younger. She continued through the rest of the leaders.

"Sysselman John Chandler, your name shall be Olaf Sigtryggson. Your mighty spear will be known as Dragon Slayer. Remember, all of you, you can only reach Valhalla and sup with the gods if you die with a weapon in your hand. It is not for those who hide at home."

"Michael, you will be Bjorn Ironside"

"You, Joe, are destined to become a mighty warrior, a berserker. You will feel no pain from any wounds. You will be fearless. Your name will be Troels, stone of Thor."

"As we now number over 40,000 members, Jarl Blood-Axe will henceforth be Konge or King Blood-Axe."

\*\*\*

On returning to his house in Newport Pagnell, Blood-Axe found a curt note from his wife and a letter from her divorce lawyer on the mantel piece. He had forty-eight hours to vacate the house. She had been reading some of the more lurid fan mail on his laptop.

After packing some of his things he contemplated the glowing amber of the thirty-year-old Macallan in its crystal glass, rolling a sip around his tongue and feeling its warmth burning into the tender cells of his palate and cheeks. *Ah well, at least there's no need to worry about the tattoos. I wonder which of my female fans I should invite round for a bit of fun?*

# CHAPTER 5

## SHIELD-MAIDENS, SORCERESSES AND VALKYRIES

A Greek chorus of old men:

*"If we give these women the least hold over us, it is all up! Their audacity will know no bounds! We will see them building ships, and fighting at sea, as Artemisia did. Nay, if they want to ride as cavalry, we had best sack the knights, for women excel in riding and have a fine, firm bottom for the gallop. Just think of all those troops of Amazons which Micon painted for us, fighting hand-to-hand with men."*

Aristophanes – Lysistrata

The existence of shield-maidens was a disputed part of Viking history until the advent of the Blood-Axe revival. Many Norse myths portray women who stood in the wall-shield and fought as warriors beside the men. They feature in several sagas including the *Volsunga Saga*. This includes Brynhildr of Wagnerian fame.

Byzantine historians recorded shield-maidens as part of the Viking force which attacked Bulgaria in 971. In modern times, female bones bearing cuts from weapons have been unearthed on several ancient battle fields, mixed in with those of other warriors.

In our own era, women fighters are still a minority, though there is plenty of evidence to deny those who say that women are too sensitive or weak for war. There were successful female fighter squadrons in the Red Air Force during Soviet Russia's Great Patriotic War against the Germans. Today, females are increasingly accepted in front line battle formations, especially in the Israeli forces. The Royal Air Force decreed that women would be allowed in close combat roles in 2017, the first to be so accepted in the UK. Increasing numbers of female officers make it through US Marine Corps training. The US deploys many woman drone pilots deployed in bunkers and willing to wipe out whole villages with bombs and missiles.

Advances in lighter-weight and remote-control weapons help make all this possible but egalitarian ideas and feminism are the main drivers. How appropriate then that women play a dominant role in the *Blood-Axe Saga*. The events in the Saga remove all doubt as to female effectiveness in the shield-wall. Some argue that women warriors are the key to understanding the events that the saga describes.

***

*"After the practice reenactments in Englaland (The original name for England), the great sorceress Freyja, much favored by Blood- Axe, recruited and trained three large bands of women with extraordinary abilities. From Olympians and other outstanding athletes she formed the Shield-maidens. They were trained in Viking and modern martial arts. All were crack shots with firearms, as well*

*as being deadly with bows, axes, spears and swords. Many Viking men trembled before them. They were bound together by oaths of sisterhood. Freyja needed more sorceresses to support her in motivating and supporting the health of the large armies that Konge Blood-Axe now commanded. He took no action without consulting her on the omens and the favor of the gods. She found many gifted and fey women among the secretive Wicca sects and healers of the UK. She taught them the ways of the Norse gods and the Vikings.*

*Lastly, came the dreaded Valkyrie. Chosen after great tests of arms, stress and endurance from the elites of the other two groups, these warrior women became Freyja's shock troops. They waited their opportunity to cut down those fleeing the shield-wall and to assassinate any opponents of Freyja and Konge Blood-Axe"*

**The Blood-Axe Saga**

\*\*\*

The Viking Council met in the torch-lit Great Mead Hall. The flickering torches painted the oak beams, weapons, shields and flags in red and gold. On a raised dais, Konge Blood-Axe presided from his gilded throne. Wearing his silvan wolf furs and the gold circlet of his crown, he looked stronger and younger than ever. The serving wenches were shooed out for this important discussion. Drinking horns went un-replenished.

Diminutive Air Vice Marshal Mike Jackson, now Bjorn Ironside, was holding forth. His blond hair shone brightly. His chin jutted out, as he expected a tough reaction, but was determined to have his say.

"Look. We all appreciate the contribution Freyja has made to the authenticity and morale of the Vikings…"

Before he could continue, there was a thumping of fists on the trestle tables in agreement. Freyja was popular, especially among the strongest and fittest of the company. She had visited all of them for steamy nights of passion, leaving them exhausted, deeply satisfied and bearing her tell-tale claw marks. These nocturnal dalliances contributed to at least three divorces. Freyja glared at Ironside and then smiled benignly around at her supporters.

Ironside waited for silence and continued. Some council members gave him flinty stares.

"You only need to see some of the so-called shield-maidens to know that they are taking massive doses of anabolic steroids. Many have those spikey lesbian haircuts and muscles like prize bulls. They have no authenticity in the Viking records. The Wicca recruits are full of mumbo jumbo and false cures. We need to kick them all out before these crazy feminists stage a coup and take over."

This elicited boos and grumbles from even more of the hundred or so Viking leaders in the room. Though some of the shield-maidens were gay and had Sapphic liaisons, many others, well trained by Freyja, held many a sturdy warrior in sexual thrall. Others were respected and mighty warriors in their own right. Blood-Axe looked sternly at Ironside. He was still his friend. Tiredly, he tried to calm things.

"Sit down Ironside! You clearly have no support for this proposal."

Muttering furiously, Ironside reluctantly resumed his place at the end of a bench among disapproving looks from his fellows.

Someone jeered at his small stature amidst appreciative laughter.

"We were still waiting for him to stand up."

Blood-Axe winced. He was quite short himself and disliked jokes about people's appearance. Freyja's face remained impassive. She made the evil eye sign towards Ironside. His forehead wrinkled with worry and he could not meet her dark eyes. Across the table, Solveig, the giant smith, ran a fat finger across his throat in an unmistakable gesture. Freyja gave him a nod.

After that night, retired Air Vice Marshal Mike Jackson, aka Bjorn Ironside was never seen again. The official line was that Freyja had consulted the gods and learned that he had chosen to leave the Vikings and the country. The lesson was not wasted on any who opposed the shield-maidens.

\*\*\*

In a large room at New Scotland Yard, heavyset and ruddy faced Detective Chief Superintendent Dirk Masher met with senior members of his anti-terrorist group. They were on edge, as he had his dander up. He tersely explained that the Home Secretary, the Minister in charge of UK security, the police and the justice system, required action. Too many people associated with the Vikings had committed apparent suicide or disappeared. The most recent to go missing was a recently retired Air Vice Marshal, Michael Jackson, aka Ironside. He was privy to still-top-secret intelligence on Russian anti-missile defenses. The RAF was desperate to locate him.

Masher paced around the table. He glared into the eyes of each in turn.

"Come on! You've all read the files. I want ideas on how to infiltrate these Viking bastards—and this week, if you please."

A butch looking female inspector piped up,

"We have records of at least ten coppers who are part-time members of the Vikings. We could get one of them to spy for us."

Masher banged a meaty fist on the table, growling menacingly. His startled team jerked upright in their seats as their pens, notepads and coffee mugs bounced.

"That won't fly. I've read their files. They're village bobbies and the like, numpties all. Besides, being cops they would automatically create suspicion. No Vikings will really trust them."

Undeterred by her boss's boorish manner, the inspector was pensive for a moment. Then she rejoined,

"We have a modern pentathlete in the squad, Juliette O'Malley. She's only a detective constable and transferred from the serious crime squad just a month ago. She's still in training, but she's aced everything so far. I was hoping she'd join my team."

Masher looked interested.

"Why her?"

"Well, here's the thing. We have several low-grade informers in the Vikings. They tell us that the senior Vikings are all male and well established, except for one.

She calls herself Freyja. She's shot to the top of the hierarchy. She's very close to this Sir Chris Walls character, aka Blood-Axe.

"She's recruiting athletes and sportswomen. They seem to be growing in influence. Several have established liaisons with Viking leaders. If we could get O'Malley into Freyja's good graces, she'd be well placed to get us what we need."

Masher looked pleased, closed the meeting and asked for Juliette O'Malley's file. He tapped his teeth with a pencil as he perused it. She was damned attractive, with twinkling blue eyes, a pale complexion, black shoulder length hair and a super-fit body. He picked up the phone.

"OK, get her in here for interview. If we delete her police files and provide a different job record, she might be able to do it."

***

Lord James Algernon Fortescue Farquhar Plummley was known as Algy to most of his circle, and Algae by those he knew at Eton. On the patio of Plummley Manor, near Hemel Hemstead, Algy and Lady Penelope Plummley were settling their ample behinds into the chintz cushions on their white wicker chairs. The bow-tied butler,

Clarence, poured more Earl Grey into their gilded Royal Doulton cups, proffering some buttered scones. They were planning a dinner gathering of interesting people.

Algy stuffed another fluffy scone into his mouth and spluttered while chewing.

"Who've we got so far?"

Lady Penelope winced at his lack of manners, but read her list aloud:

"Dinner Invitations for the 14<sup>th</sup> of October.

Princess Beatrix – Declined - *Stuck up Bitch.*

Sir John and Lady Nettlewood - Joint owners of Nettlewood Construction. - Accepted

The Honorable Hughie Dagwood and friend. - *He's gay and a hoot. You remember. We met them at the Queen's garden party.* - Accepted

The right honorable Andrew Blenkinsop MP, Minister of Transport and friend. - *It's his secretary. Wifie's not to know. We need his help diverting the high-speed railway line away from the woods just beyond the east gate.* - Accepted

General Sir John Fraser, Military Cross, Distinguished Service Order and Bar and Lady Fraser. - Accepted

Wally Troutbeck and Mrs. Troutbeck. She's the artist and

he's the author. - Accepted

Prince Ogulu Ogalu, heir to the throne of Balotoland and two wives. - Accepted

*Weren't you his fag at Eton Algy and where exactly is Balotoland?"*

"Christ don't remind me about Eton. The silly arse insisted I warm his pajamas in front of the common-room fire every winter's night. If that wasn't enough, I had to sit on the toilet seat to warm that for him too. My bottom was blue some nights. As for *Blatu Baltu* or where ever, I have absolutely no idea, presumably Africa somewhere?"

"Why do you keep in touch with such bullies Algy?"

"It's the Eton system darling. We all became bullies in turn. It was never anything personal."

"Mmm, if you say so, Algy. Well we want two more guests. Any ideas?"

He glanced at a headline in the London Times which lay on the table.

"This Viking reenactment fella, Blood-Axe, is getting in the news a lot. Maybe he'd liven things up a little; and perhaps this Freyja woman. She looks very sexy and claims to be some sort of witch."

Lady Penelope looked over her spectacles doubtfully and raised a perfectly groomed eyebrow in his direction.

# CHAPTER 6

## PROTECTING THE KING

*"Stoop, Romans, Stoop and let us bathe our hands in Caesar's blood*

*Up to the elbows and besmear our swords*

*Then walk we forth, even to the marketplace.*

*And waving our red weapons o'er our heads, Let us all cry,*

*Peace! Freedom! Liberty!"*

Brutus - In Julius Caesar - William Shakespeare

In her recently built Seers' Hall, Freyja was ensconced on a black panther skin laid across her ebonite chair. In contrast to Blood-Axe's Great Mead Hall, with all its colorful weapons, banners and shields, her lair was painted matte black throughout and open solely to her female devotees. The last male to enter had been found flayed, emasculated and hanging upside down from a remote oak in the wood. The men kept well away now. His body was fed to the wild boar.

The enormous pale orb of a full moon was depicted high at one gable-end of the hall in eerily luminous paint. Freyja's attendant shield-maidens wore black leather surcoats. Their rippling arms and necks were tattooed with dark runic inscriptions. Night camouflage cream was smeared thickly around their eyes.

The sorceresses passed around "magic" potions, comprising secret herbs, selected fungi and anabolic steroids laced with sugar and a goodly amount of vodka.

Their hair hung in long uncombed tangles of bleached white. The ragged remains of shrouds hid their true shapes. All their faces were a uniform and expressionless alabaster due to a paste-like make-up.

Above, in the minstrels' gallery, six white-robed blind sisters played nonstop weird music. Two blew drones, instruments fashioned by twisting three cow horns together, venting wheezing groans. Another sister plucked a primitive lyre-like instrument with reverberating twangs. The other two clacked sticks against split pieces of wood. The whole cacophony was accompanied by sinister wailing and growling from their throats, to a background like an overloaded cart clattering down a rocky path. Those listening below were transported to drug induced heaven or hell, according to Freyja's mood and direction.

Two seers hustled in a tall, well-built woman in white damask from the side of the room and onto Freyja's platform. The gathering looked towards her expectantly. A veil hid the newcomer's identity.

The beat of the drums and caterwauling reached a crescendo. It stopped abruptly. The unmistakable sickly stench of fresh bulls' blood pervaded the room, released from storage tanks on the roof. Matte-black tiled channels in the walls ran red with it. The shield-maidens emitted a collective roar. Some bared teeth sharpened to ivory needle points and ran to the walls, lapping up blood like vampire bats.

The veil was whipped off the stalwart, pale novitiate. She stood erect, then bowed her head before mighty Freyja. Dropping her robe, she was pale and naked. Freyja arose from her chair. Contrived lighting made her enormous shadow sway and dance behind her. She seemed like a huge giant to those below the stage.

Freyja howled like a wolf. Even the bravest of her horde felt the hairs rise on the backs of their necks. Then they echoed her cries. Far off in the darkened woods, a patrolling Viking sentry heard the pandemonium and trembled, gripping tightly to the hilt of his sword.

Freyja raised a hand, cutting off the din. She let the dead silence build expectation and tension as her dark eyes flashed around the room. Her voice rang out, shattering the stillness.

"Juliette O'Malley, do you swear to obey the laws of Odin and our gods, on pain of hideous, lingering death,"

"I do."

"Do you vow never to betray our sacred sisterhood here gathered?"

"I so vow."

"Hold out your arm."

As O'Malley stretched out her arm, Freyja seized it,

digging her black claws into the wrist and twisting it upward. Handed a glowing branding iron, she seared it deep into the muscular forearm. She looked with cruel pleasure directly into the unflinching blue eyes. O'Malley gasped and almost fainted with the waves of excruciating pain but tried to stare her out. Then her eyes screwed tight. She gasped in agony. She barely heard Freyja pronounce,

"These runes spell your new name. You will henceforth be Aegea. She was an Amazon queen. Carry her spirit with pride."

\*\*\*

Chief Superintendent Masher was reading a file in his office. There was a photograph on his desk. It was him, years previously, a ruggedly handsome firearms officer in full SWAT team gear. There was no sign of his present booze raddled complexion. Masher felt the vibration of his cell phone. He glanced down at the simple text message.

*"I'm in."*

\*\*\*

On the 16th hole at Little Linford Golf Course, Blood-Axe was playing his usual poor round. His bodyguard was his nephew, Joe the Berserker. He stood close behind him as he went to take a shot from the edge of a clump of trees. Once a nerdy weakling, Joe was utterly transformed since their visit to Norway. He was now strong as an ox and completely fearless. Freyja had named him as a Ber-serkr or bear warrior. The Icelandic *Ynglinga Saga* describes such doughty fighters. They drew their strength and courage from their bear cult. They felt no pain in battle, often eschewing protective mail shirts for bear, wolf or boar skins.

As Blood-Axe swung to take his shot, a meticulously aimed arrow whistled past his ear. It thudded deep into the sycamore trunk behind him. His nephew Joe the Berserker, renamed Troels, gave an enormous roar. His eyes seemed to be on fire. Raising a round shield in front of his lord, he stood ready to protect him from further arrows. There were none.

\*\*\*

That night, in Blood-Axe's private quarters, Freyja held out the arrow dug from the tree. She called for Bone Cruncher, one of his massive wolfhounds. It bounded over to her, wagging its tail and licking her tattooed hand

and black nails. She scratched its paw with the arrow tip. Bone Cruncher leapt back, yelping. Giving her a reproachful look, and whimpering. It keeled over, stone dead. The Konge gasped.

"Yes, my liege lord. It was poisoned. We can't risk your person with just a single bodyguard anymore. From now on, the strongest of my shield-maidens should protect you at all times."

He looked doubtful. Some of the women seemed as though they might tear him asunder rather than keep him safe. Still, others were wickedly attractive.

"OK, send me the ones you propose, but I get to pick those I want."

***

A week later, Aegea, aka Detective Constable O'Malley, smiled as she texted Masher.

*"The boss is in me."*

She chuckled at the thought of him puzzling over the meaning of the message. She hoped it made him stew. He had made a pass at her during the interview. She had made a joke of it, but he disgusted her. Yuk! He had a face like a raddled Galapagos iguana.

She omitted informing him how her bowshot, which narrowly missed Blood-Axe, had won the trust of Freyja.

Freyja repaid Aegea in two ways. One was to make her one of the four new shield-maidens in the Royal Close Protection Squad. The other was a real eye-opener.

Aegea thought she was sexually as straight as a die. There had been overtures from some women police officers, with no effect.

Now, under the influence of some potion of Freyja's, she enjoyed one of the best nights of wild sex she could remember. Freyja was amazing. Aegea craved more of the same from that lithe and supple body. Maybe she was falling for this powerful angel of darkness.

# CHAPTER 7

## GOOD COP, BAD COP, EVEN WORSE COP

來到我們這裡的敵人的間諜必須被尋找，受到賄賂的誘惑，被帶走並舒適地安置。因此，他們將成為轉換間諜，可用於我們的服務。

*The enemy's agents who have come to spy on us must be sought out, tempted with bribes, led away and housed comfortably. Then, they will become converted spies and available for our service.*

**Sun Tzu- The Art of War 孫子戰爭的藝術**

The guests were arriving at Plummley Hall for the dinner party. As the chauffeurs opened the limo doors for them, Freyja and Blood-Axe made their melodramatic entrance on horseback.

Several heavy horses and their wild riders burst from the woods at the gallop. The guard of four shield-maidens and Troels the Berserker all wore full Viking gear and weapons. Their heavy round shields hung on the horses' rumps from their saddles. Freyja was dressed in a black leather jerkin that pushed her cleavage up. Her long dark tresses flew behind her. Blood-Axe looked huge, swaddled in wolf furs. His hair and beard were braided around human finger bones obtained from a medical supplies firm.

The other guests stopped in their tracks as the horses skidded to a halt, their braking hooves sprayed gravel from the driveway. The Vikings leapt from their steeds. The Konge and Freyja marched straight past the open-mouthed guests and up the steps to the hall. Their guards peeled off, hefting their shields and spears. They stood menacingly, stony-faced, looking down at the guests from their posts either side of the doorway.

Lord and Lady Plummley smiled politely from their open door. They were a vision of elegance. He sported a purple crushed-velvet jacket with grey trousers and a yellow silk cravat. She wore a diamond necklace and bracelet to complement her white harem pants and green silk top. He stepped forward in welcome.

"King Blood-Axe and Freyja, I presume. How nice to see you both! Do come in. Let our butler, Clarence, take your er...furs, and perhaps the um…weapons?"

Blood-Axe rudely shouldered past him with a grunt, ignoring Lady P. With his usual aplomb, Clarence led him to the reception room. When he tried to relieve Blood-Axe of the weapons, he backed away rapidly from the withering look the Konge threw him.

Meanwhile, Freyja gave Lady P an openly lustful look that made her blush and step back. When Lord P gallantly kissed Freyja's hand, she seized his. Thrusting her other into his groin, she gave him a little squeeze. He gasped, but looked quite pleased.

"Well, er...welcome! I can see that we are in for an interesting evening."

\*\*\*

In Thames Valley police's sub-police station off Newport Pagnell High Street, police constable Fred Grimby was engaged in a row with his station sergeant.

"Look Fred, we've both known Chris Walls for over five years. He's a pillar of the local community, a close friend of the Mayor and well respected in the Home Office. These allegations of yours are frankly ridiculous."

"But Sarg…"

"Listen, I'm not saying these oldsters don't go in for a bit of laddish fun. Maybe they break a few minor laws from time to time, but look at the business they've brought to the town. We'd be very unpopular if we charged them with rape, kidnapping, grievous bodily harm and conspiracy, as you suggest. Now why don't you go home to Marge and the kids and be a good lad. I'll hold on to this report for now."

As soon as constable Grimby left his room the sergeant tossed the document into the bin. Unseen, a figure watched from the darkness beyond the glass wall of the office.

\*\*\*

Rural England is partly policed by special constables. These tend to be somewhat officious or alternatively public-spirited individuals who like to play at policemen in their spare time. Special Constable Albert, "nosey" Parker, was such a man. He felt his life was devoid of meaning after Aston Martin shut its production plant in the village and ended his job in the stores. Nowadays, he loved handing out parking tickets to irate motorists, warning kids not to ride bikes on the sidewalk and pretending to his neighbors that he knew everything going on in the underworld.

He was also a junior member of the Vikings, hanging round the edge of the serious players. A wonderful opportunity now presented itself. He often waited till the Sergeant had left before rifling through the bins for some tidbit of scandal to impress his wife and friends. Today, his eyes opened wide as he read the allegations about the Vikings. He could get some real value out of this, but how best to handle it?

\*\*\*

Back at Plummley Hall, the festivities were about to begin. One of the liveried flunkies in crimson knickerbockers, a frogged coat and a powdered wig, tried to hand Blood-Axe a scotch. It was in a fancy glass, blown in 1715 and engraved with, *To the king over the water* i.e. James the second, "the old pretender." The Konge hurled the rare antique and its contents into the fireplace. As the glass smashed, the spirit burst into a ball of flame. Grabbing the decanter, he poured the entire contents into a horn he kept hung by his side, spilling some on the exquisite silk Persian rug.

Turning to a concerned Lord P, he pulled a bottle of Blood-Axe mead from a bag hanging from his belt. Dumping it on the table, he grunted,

"A presi for you. Can't stand the stuff miself."

Blood-Axe swigged from his horn and let out a loud belch. Spying Fennella, the mistress of the Right Honorable minister, he goosed her. She giggled and stroked the finger bones twisted into his beard. Her man stood well back, aghast.

Meanwhile, Freyja deftly spiked all the drinks with some potion of her own. She had an arm around Lady P and was openly fondling her left breast.

Clarence, the butler, regained some of his usual poise and announced.

"My Lord, Ladies and gentlemen, dinner is served."

His lip curled slightly on the "gentlemen," as he glanced

at Blood-Axe, who sat down before the ladies were seated. The oaf then picked up the Royal Albert soup bowl and slurped his way through the contents.

Freyja was wiggling her toes under the table into Prince Ogulu Ogalu's crotch. He shifted in his seat savoring the moment. He yelled down the table,

"Ahoy there! Algae, this is your best party ever!"

Blood-Axe and Freyja proceeded to scarf down the pheasant using their fingers. He seized a tasty morsel from Lady P's plate, whom was sat next to him. Taken aback, she was uncertain how to react until he used her hair to wipe the grease from his fingers. She shrieked, but then Freyja's drugs kicked in and everything seemed cool and exactly as it should be.

The Honorable Hughie Dagwood winked at his partner, Alan, and dug into his food with his hands.

"I say what fun, Plummers old boy. Come on. Be a sport, let's all be Vikings tonight. Hey! King Blood-Axe, can we become Vikings too?"

Blood-Axe rose up from the table, knocking some priceless porcelain onto the floor. He looked green around the gills and rushed to a window, throwing up over the silk curtains before resuming his seat.

Freyja answered for the Konge, with a wicked smile that left her eyes coldly observing Hughie.

"Course you can join us. You and Alan come and see me, I'll fix you up."

The right honorable Andrew Blenkinsop MP, Minister of Transport, was still angry about the Konge flirting with his mistress. He decided to confide in General Sir John Fraser, who was muttering something unintelligible next to him. He whispered in his ear,

"Don't worry General. Entre nous, the PM told me we have a police informer in the Vikings and they'll all be in jail before long."

The General, rather deaf, and stoned out of his mind, bellowed,

"You have a police informer in the Vikings you say? What on earth for? Thish is the besht party I've been to for years. Yippeee! Pour me shome more of that wine. Itsh shplendid."

Freyja gave them a dark look, making a mental note of the outburst. Blood-Axe, taking umbrage at the Minister's whispering, leapt to his feet. He smashed an axe into the Eton Mess desert. It spurted out either side of the blade. The Minister received a face full of whipped cream, meringue and strawberries. The Konge grabbed the table with both hands and turned it over, sending food and more family heirlooms crashing everywhere. He head-butted Clarence when the butler rushed forward. The butler crumpled to the ground in a heap.

In the early light of dawn, most of the guests lay sprawled unconscious in various states of disarray around the wreckage of the dining room and up the grand staircase. Some bore distinctive claw marks.

On a couch in the hallway, the Minister of Transport lay smiling between the Prince's two naked wives. He snored loudly as Freyja and Blood-Axe took their leave.

She hooked Blood-Axe's arm to pass through the front door, turning her head to the semi-comatose Lord Plummley, who lay flat out on a rug by the front door.

"Thank you for a perfectly splendid evening Algy. Let's do it again. It was such fun."

The noble lord felt as though a vice was crushing his skull. He just groaned.

\*\*\*

In New Scotland Yard, Chief Superintendent Masher was listening to the lowly special constable across his desk. He masked his mounting irritation with a smile. What could he possibly learn from such amateur minions?

Albert "nosey" Parker had explained the cover-up taking place in Newport Pagnell police station. He showed Fred Grimby's crumpled allegations. He offered to investigate the Vikings further. The Chief Super feigned a pleased smile, much to Parker's satisfaction. He left, preening himself.

As soon as he was out of the door Masher arranged a conversation with Aegea, aka DC O'Malley. He needed to warn her that there was a rather stupid loose cannon on her patch. He would advise a course of action.

\*\*\*

The day after the party, Freyja called her most trusted Valkyries, seers and shield-maidens to her hall. Her eyes flashed with anger.

"Sisters, we have police spies amongst our band."

Aegea tensed, feeling cold fingers grasping her heart. She noted that Freyja was not looking at her. She forced herself to be calm by controlling her breathing.

"You, my most trusted ones, must seek them out, but take no action. Report them to me. Now go. Use your sex, your guile and your potions on the men to discover the traitors. They will be punished."

\*\*\*

The next day, Freyja met a Colombian friend from school at Heathrow London Airport.

As the Colombian girl walked out of flight arrivals at London's Heathrow Airport, Freyja looked around for anyone watching. She'd been there a while, constantly checking for under cover observers. There were only the body-armored uniformed officers, bristling with Tasers, pistols and assault rifles. They strolled stolidly past without glancing at the Colombian. Freyja signaled to her to follow.

In the car park she turned, checking that they were not observed. She sat the girl in the seat of her hire-car and finally spoke.

"Did you bring me the borrachero?"

"Si Doña Freyja. Do you have the money?"

"Of course."

Freyja drove them in silence into a country lane. There they exchanged a package for a bundle of cash. Freyja drove back towards Heathrow and dropped her friend at the nearest underground station.

Borrachero is also known as the Devil's Breath in Colombia. It is derived from the seeds of a tree flower. The trumpet-like white bloom emits sweet scents in the evenings to attract nocturnal pollinators. In some countries it is called Rena de la noche, Queen of the night.

When administered to an unwitting victim, Borrachero induces a trance-like state. The subject becomes totally obedient, almost like a zombie, but retains the appearance of normality.

\*\*\*

Aegea's subsequent call with Masher was disturbing. He ordered her to betray the two informers from Thames Valley Police to the Viking leaders.

"It'll build credibility with Blood-Axe and Freyja. Besides, they're just pawns in our game."

She could see the logic behind this, but it went against all her training. She had a sense of loyalty to fellow coppers. Masher was horrible. By contrast, she enjoyed her close relationship with the Konge. He was witty, intelligent and quite handsome really. His rages were usually play-acting. He often sought her out as his bedmate. The sex was not bad either.

Aegea's affair with Freyja was also becoming much more serious. Were the torrid tangling of their sweating limbs on the wolf furs, the screaming climaxes and soft caresses, the result of mounting feelings of love? She doubted it was mutual. Her loyalties were torn. She would consider how to handle things. Meantime, she followed up on the Chief Super's information, taking steps to locate and investigate the two policemen he considered dispensable pawns.

***

It was a winter dawning. In the exhausted happiness of sated lust, Freyja looked down on the sleeping Aegea with fondly caressing eyes. She knew every inch of that lithe powerful body. As she pulled on a gown against the chill, she realized that something was amiss. *Aegea seems worried about something. Her sleep was disturbed. Well, we'll find out what's troubling her.*

Freyja walked over to the scullery and prepared a refreshing morning drink for her lover. She raised a finger on an afterthought and added a little clear liquid from a vial on her shelf. Returning to Aegea, she tenderly stroked the silk-soft skin of her shoulders

"Come my love, drink this. It's morning and we have things to do."

Mumbling sleepily, Aegea smiled at her and sipped the drink. Her dark pupils grew to enormous size and she felt utter devotion and obedience to Freyja.

Freyja cradled Aegea's head in her arm, gently stroking her lips with a black finger nail. She began to ask questions. Aegea felt compelled to answer.

\*\*\*

In the Great Mead Hall, Blood-Axe noticed Aegea's pupils almost subsuming her blue irises. He was not feeling well himself. *It's as though I've lost control.*

His twenty most trusted House-Karls watched in grim silence as Freyja and Aegea mercilessly prepared the ritual death of the Blood Eagle for the two policemen, Special Constable, Albert, "nosey" Parker and Police Constable Fred Grimby of Thames Valley's Newport Pagnell station. They gurgled on their own blood. Freyja had had their tongues torn out lest they compromise her lover.

Each man was tied, leaning forward over a wooden beam at chest height. They were stripped to the waist and sweating with the strain of their leather bonds and with a terrible fear. They could not scream their protests, but their biceps and their neck muscles knotted, fit to burst.

Blood-Axe puzzled as to why he, a civilized man, was taking it all so calmly. Inside, he found it deeply distressing, but his presence was expected. Sometimes, he wished he had stuck to golf, or that his name was Rubber-Axe. He quaffed a stiff Malt whiskey to stiffen his resolve. The strong spirit interacted with whatever Freyja regularly added to his food. He felt dulled to it all, listless and tired.

He nodded for his women to begin the ritual. Examples had to be made, at least according to Freyja. He managed to look away when the horror began.

Aegea was as though in a dream, controlled by Freyja. Moving in complete synchronization they both coldly rocked razor-sharp axe blades to slice apart the ribs of each man on either side of his spine. The ribs were peeled back and bloodied lungs gently eased out. They were spread either side of them over the beams like ghastly wings. The men writhed and twitched, tearing at their chains. Finally, they died, gasping in the utter agony of the Blood Eagle.

The Vikings observed the lessons of what they had seen. It was death to traitors. The power of Blood-Axe was absolute. When the others had filed out in silence, the gore-soaked Freyja and Aegea sated their slippery lust in a threesome with the Konge. The thrill of the murders proved an irresistible aphrodisiac to Freyja.

Later, Freyja mused to herself as she untangled her sweat-sticky, blood-crusted limbs from those of the others. *Aegea is mine forever now. I'll keep her close and her channels to the anti-terrorist force open. They should prove most useful.*

\*\*\*

Masher sat happily contemplating the reports of the disappearance of the two men from Thames Valley Police on his computer screen. Muttering, "Good Girl," he sent a note to the relevant personnel to advise that his department would be in charge of the investigation. No one questioned matters of national security. Then, he encrypted and redacted all the files so that no one could ever read them.

# CHAPTER 8

## FOREIGN AFFAIRS

*"The fame of Konge Blood-Axe and his Viking hordes spread throughout the world. All those with the questing, restless Viking spirit flocked to his banners. Many had true Viking blood, but opportunists and knaves came with avarice and evil in their hearts. Foreign rulers sought to send spies amongst the Vikings. With the aid of our ancient gods, they were all confounded."*

The Blood-Axe Saga

Konge Blood-Axe was attending a presentation to the Viking Council. A young and rather weedy Harvard MBA, self-consciously wearing full Viking garb, was explaining how the movement had become increasingly international. Blood-Axe marveled that the Scandinavian countries had all formed thriving chapters of his organization founded in Britain. *Maybe their leadership left them centuries before to go exploring and pillaging. That would've left only the boring and tedious behind.* He remembered working a year in Denmark. *They were all so damn civilized and dull.*

The MBA used his laser pen to point to the strength of various Viking chapters on his world map.

"As you might expect, Northern Europe, including Germany, Belgium and the Netherlands have the highest density of members. Though look here, Normandy, other parts of France, Switzerland and Austria show quite well.

"The big surprise is Russia. As you've read, the cause has been enthusiastically taken up and become a political party. It's winning seats in local elections.

"Across the US, there are many chapters, especially amongst the biker gangs of California, here."

Blood-Axe, grumped at him as he tapped the screen,

"Yes, we know where California is. Get on with it!"

The MBA rushed nervously on.

"Well, er… As you know, one gang was already called the Vikings. Their membership has burgeoned. In recent clashes, they have wrested dominance from the Hells Angels.

"We have also attracted an unusual number of recruits in Minnesota. They have a well-known American football team called the Vikings. Their fans are signing up en-masse.

"Now I'd like to put up some of the issues and threats from the global expansion.

"The Council needs to consider how it can keep control of all these affiliate chapters. One concern is that there is a backlash, especially in Germany and the US, due to infiltration by Nazi and Ku Klux Klan elements. The last thing we can afford is to remove our friendly mask and become classed as right-wing terrorists."

Freyja looked inscrutable. In her view that could be excellent sport and exactly aligned with her plans.

Blood-Axe wrinkled his brow—worried. *How did what had begun with such fun and frolics become so damnably problematic?* He mused, *It was only a few years back that the US tore down its statues of Southern generals as symbols of racism and slavery. Some fools in Sweden have proposed eradicating the Vikings from their culture as representing savagery incompatible with modern bland humanism. All we wanted to do was to live a little fantasy to relieve the boredom of old age. How did it come to this?*

Freyja paid rapt attention throughout the PowerPoint show, tapping a few notes into her iPhone. Carried away by the numbers shown, the Finance Director calculated the hundreds of millions that all the global activity was bringing in.

After a general discussion, the Konge retired to his private chambers with just a few trusted advisors and his bodyguards.

"Come on through, I want to discuss action steps."

\*\*\*

Freyja easily persuaded the Konge and his inner circle to let her and her shield-maidens deal with any dissonant elements internationally. Blood-Axe looked relieved. *Glad she's around. Hate having to deal with all that. It's no fun at all.*

For her part, she was surprised how easily her forces were given carte blanche to dominate the world-wide organization. The others must be stupid.

\*\*\*

To make the whole enterprise more politically correct, she initiated a campaign to recruit ethnic minorities. This was surprisingly successful. One result was a thriving Zulu branch, and several other chapters in Africa. There was a Gurkha following in Nepal, Pashtuns in Afghanistan and some rather sexy tattooed Maoris in New Zealand.

She called Blood-Axe from her private plane over the Atlantic. The success of the business and her international role allowed her this extravagance.

"The diversity program helps to deter most racist elements. If there were any around, no one asks too many questions as to where to or why they disappear. Besides, in the US, the crime wave from biker gangs has diminished significantly.

"Our PR agency has devised a new slogan,

**"Be a Viking! It's a way of life, not Racism."**

\*\*\*

The laboratory of TPY plasma plc operated within an extensive high-security site near Cranfield Technology Park, close to Newport Pagnell. Its ownership, through shell companies in Lichtenstein, could not be traced to the Vikings. Freyja kept its existence secret from Blood-Axe and the others in the leadership.

There were clean-rooms in a large modern building. To get into the positive pressure environment the workers had to pass through airlocks. Lab assistants in white, all-enveloping dust protective suits and gloves handled the most sensitive electronic components with great care in a separate assembly area. In another space, highly educated and skilled artificial intelligence experts programmed various pieces of equipment at their workstations.

The cover story, which the junior employees actually believed, was that they were working on top secret engine management systems for some of the Formula 1 car racing teams. Most of the international firms based their engineering teams in the area.

Those TPY plasma employees with any idea of what was really going on were sworn to secrecy. More importantly, they were only too aware of what would happen to anyone who let slip even the slightest fragment of information. Disappearances were frequent. The pay was excellent and the work at the cutting edge.

Select technicians began their day with an elevator ride to corridors and large laboratories fifty feet below the main building. There, encased in concrete, were locations for top secret experiments. Freyja often visited to oversee the work. There they developed cyborgs which mixed characteristics of living creatures with electronics. There were also advanced experiments with robots. Technicians worked on humanoid forms. There were titanium ribs and other bones in various stages of assembly, along with wiring and circuit boards in seeming disarray.

\*\*\*

From a thick hedgerow a couple of fields away from the laboratory perimeter a middle-aged birdwatcher trained her binoculars on a bullfinch further up the hedge. She elbowed aside the prickly brambles and nettles with the thick green sleeves of her Barbour to get a better view.

"There, perfect!"

Halfway across the field, a ruddy-faced farmer dragged a harrow over the earth with his bright blue tractor. As he drove in straight lines, the heavy steel frame of the harrow pressed its serried metal-spikes down into the lumpy soil. It broke up the clods and scratched out the roots of any weeds. He found it deeply satisfying, striping the brown earth with perfect corduroy striations. The sun was shining. The air was fresh. Townies had no idea of the pleasures of farming. Life was good. He smiled happily, thinking of the coming night in the Great Mead Hall with his Viking friends.

Enjoying the early morning sunshine, a birder brushed a stray hair from her face. *It needs cutting and coloring. It must have been months since the last time. Must get it done.* She looked up from under the narrow brim of her dark-green waterproofed hat at the clear blue sky and gasped. A huge raptor was soaring high above. *It couldn't be? I must be mistaken. The nearest golden eagles are hundreds of miles away in Scotland, and rare enough even there.*

She excitedly adjusted the focus on her Nikon binoculars as she ticked off the field identification points in her head. *Broad but long wings. Separated feathers like fingers reaching beyond the wing to sense for thermals. A fanned-out tail. Powerful beak for tearing prey. Dark brown overall, with a golden sheen on the head feathers.*

*This eagle must be an escapee from a bird park, but there are no leather traces used by the handler to hold the bird on their arm. It's a puzzle.*

The giant bird spotted her from a mile away. It circled closer on its eight-foot wings without losing altitude.

In a tree behind the birder, and in her blind spot, was an even stranger sight for the UK. A chunkily built Harpy Eagle from the South American rain forests grasped a branch with powerful talons, watching her intently. The heaviest eagle in the world, the Harpy weaves deftly between the rainforest trees to seize large monkeys from the boughs.

Its baleful yellow eyes, mounted in an extraordinarily large grey head, topped with a tall double crest of upright feathers, followed her every move. With an incredible burst of speed, its white underside a blur, it hurled itself from above. A couple of swift beats of stubby wings, and steering tightly with its banded tail, it was upon her in seconds. She felt a sudden shock of the impact from behind. Razor-sharp talons pierced her skull through the hat. A white flash electrified her whole being. The momentum crashed her to the ground, dead.

The Harpy was about to rip into her flesh with its steely hooked beak. Something in its brain gave it a nudge. Flapping back to its tree in a more leisurely fashion, it resumed its perch, watching.

From a bank of monitors in the security room of TPY plasma, the bird-handler was calming her racing heart after the action. She was well-pleased with her bird's performance. Her PhD from Cambridge combined Neurology and Artificial Intelligence.

In the field outside the lab, the farmer became alert and listened for a few seconds to the chattering in his earpiece. Then, he chugged the tractor over to the hedgerow. Wearing his green rubber boots, he slowly clambered down from his cab. He stepped over a dry ditch and pushed through the undergrowth to the place directed by his controller. Seizing the birder's body by the ankles, he roughly dragged it though the nettles, returning to retrieve her bloodied hat.

"Come on now mi dear. We can't leave you lying about here now, can we?"

Dumping her sprawling across the frame of the harrow behind the tractor, he tossed the hat on top. Next, he calmly trundled back towards his barn. That was where he kept the wood chipper and the cement mixer.

\*\*\*

The ceremonial duties of his court continued to pall with Blood-Axe. *What happened to the carefree Viking life? I nearly burst out laughing yesterday when I had to meet that delegation of Vegan Vikings from Osaka. Where's the logic in Vegan Vikings? I was expected to share a disgusting meal of seaweed, noodles and tofu. Yuk! All that silly bowing! It's utter nonsense!*

He chuckled when discussing it with Aegea afterwards over an especially juicy steak and a couple of bottles of red wine. For her part, Aegea felt a strong bond developing between them. The sex was good, and she liked his laconic humor. Despite all the goings-on he was a good man. Freyja was manipulating him along with everyone else. *I'm in lust with Freyja, but increasingly in love with Blood-Axe. My Viking job is to protect his person, but I'd rather protect him in every sense. Freyja worries me more every day.*

Of greater concern, because of past loyalties, was her decreasing allegiance to the horrible Masher and the Police in general. They were merely protecting a corrupt and undeserving establishment. They had scant respect for the law in doing it. Her sleep was disturbed by increasing internal conflicts and moral dilemmas.

\*\*\*

About this time Freyja introduced Reginúlfr, or Ranulf

(wolf decision), to the council. He was a man mountain. Six-feet-six-inches tall, with a broad muscular chest and massive biceps. His legs were tree trunks, knotted with muscle. His ice-blue eyes had a strange vacuity about them.

Ranulf immediately made his mark by winning the international all arms contest at the World Viking Convention in Houston. His aim seemed unerring. Every throwing axe, spear and arrow landed exactly in the center of his targets. In the freestyle fighting, his opponents were battered to the ground in minutes. No one could stand before him.

Blood-Axe felt immensely jealous. Besides his skills as a warrior, Ranulf was unbeatable at chess and any other game set before him. *To cap it all, he has the ideal blond and craggy good looks of the archetypical Hollywood Viking. He's become Freyja's constant companion. Rumor is he's her favorite lover too. I detest the great, muscle-bound lump.*

\*\*\*

In a secure room at CIA headquarters in Langley, Virginia, the top strategy team discussed the Vikings. The Deputy director shared his big idea,

"These Viking guys are everywhere, in all countries and most professions. If we can infiltrate and control them, we can use the organization as a base for our operations all over the world. Fit young CIA agents should make ideal recruits for them. It should be easy.

"Come up with a plan, by Monday."

# CHAPTER 9

## THE RAID ON OLNEY

*"Then rode mighty Blood-Axe and his army into the town of Olney. They fought, burned, ravished, and carried off a vast fortune. Many enemies were slaughtered amongst much wailing."*

The Blood-Axe Saga

The quaint and ancient village of Olney used to lie on the river Great Ouse, a few miles down-stream from Newport Pagnell. Founded in the 9<sup>th</sup> Century, it was once a border town between Saxon and Viking lands.

Tourists and locals flocked to Olney. It possessed picturesque honey-stone houses, friendly pubs, a market square, a famous church with a tall spire and a number of thatched cottages. It was a peaceful place. There, farmers gathered, country solicitors and doctors had their premises. From here, office workers commuted to Bedford, Milton Keynes, Northampton and London. People came into the weekly farmers' market to buy fresh produce, to gossip and visit the coffee shops. Alas, all that is as it used to be.

\*\*\*

Aegea, aka, Detective Constable O'Malley, sneaked into Newport Pagnell to make a surreptitious phone call to Chief Inspector Masher. She felt it was an important message. She hid around the back of a building and used a burner phone.

"You're not going to believe this, Sir."

"Try me."

"They're planning a raid on a village called Olney. They mean to raze it to the ground!"

Doubtfully, he brought up Google maps on his computer screen. A couple more clicks revealed pictures and a few facts. About 8,000 people lived there.

"You're right, I don't believe you. Someone's having you on."

Annoyed, she became insistent.

"Look, I'm risking my neck bringing you this. They're dead serious. I've heard them planning. Blood-Axe's against the idea, but Freyja and Olaf are driving forward with the plans regardless. They see it as some sort of test of Viking credentials. They're egging each other on."

"Sounds unlikely but get me some proof and we'll consider what to do."

He pushed back his swivel chair. Zooming in on the map he tapped his teeth with a pencil. *I wonder?* Pressing a button on his intercom, he called his secretary.

"Janice, have my driver bring the Jag round please. I'm taking a little trip into the country."

\*\*\*

Aegea stood next to Blood-Axe in his private meeting chamber, feigning disinterest. She sensed his irritation was mounting as he listened to the obvious rivalry between Freyja and Olaf. Each wanted to lead the raid on Olney and was pushing their own agenda.

Freyja was on her feet, pacing backwards and forwards. She chopped the air with her hand to emphasize her points. Her attention was on the Konge, desperate to convince him to back her.

Our younger Vikings want more than reenactments. You should hear the way they talk. Unless we do something, they'll drift away, back to football and pub fights on Friday nights. If we have a real raid it'll make them feel they've achieved something and bind them together."

Olaf Sigtryggson, aka John Chandler, snorted and sat up in his chair.

"No one here knows more about how combat pulls a team together than I do. Remember. I fought in

Afghanistan while Freyja was selling spells and charms in local markets. Leave this to me. The men need to bond. The girls can stay here and get a feast ready."

She hissed at him, eyes flashing in fury, but before she could say more the Konge interrupted in his sternest voice.

"Fun and mock battles are one thing. Real violence and damage to property are another. We've got a good thing going here. Those who want it are making pots of money. Both of you have leadership positions, thousands of followers and endless prestige. What I'm hearing could bring it all crashing down. If the lads and lasses want violence, let 'em go to soccer matches. Now leave me. I need to think. Aegea, you stay please."

Looking daggers at each other Freyja and Olaf stomped out.

***

In Olney Church, the vicar looked glumly down from her pulpit. Her sparse Sunday congregation comprised mainly older women. It reflected the increasing secularism across the UK. A majority still defined themselves as Christians but she divided them into the superstitious, those who were in it for social reasons, precious few real believers, and even fewer who lived the faith. Most of the population of Olney only ever attended church for baptisms, marriages and funerals. Of course, whenever the BBC broadcast *Songs of Praise* from the church, it was packed with a pious congregation, all dressed up and hoping to be on TV. Some didn't even know the words to the hymns.

Several neighboring parishes could support only visiting ministries. There just were not enough worshipers to go around anymore. Churches were closing all over England. If the lead flashing was stolen from the roof, there was no way any parish would be able to raise the funds to keep going.

She noted a huge muscular man with an unkempt beard standing next to a tiny, mousy woman, presumably his wife. His hands were scarred and as thick as sausages. The wife must have dragged him along. There was something disturbing about the way he was looking at her.

Solveig, the Viking smith, was bored. He did what many regular churchgoing men did. He scanned the audience for attractive women. It was a forlorn hope. Maybe the vicar was the best available. She wore no make-up, but the gentle swelling of her black shirt below the clerical collar seemed quite erotic. Devoid of make-up, her face was quite pretty. He entertained lascivious thoughts. Thereafter, she featured in his fantasies and dreams.

\*\*\*

Freyja persuaded Blood-Axe that the planned raid on Olney would be a rowdy but peaceful event, with lots of shouting but no real violence. It would keep the Vikings in the news, entertain the rambunctious elements and bring tourists to the town thereafter, a win-win for all concerned.

The plot she hatched with Ranulf revealed very different intentions.

"Ranulf, we'll have Solveig, the smith, ensure that the rubber guards are removed from all the weapons. You can give him my orders.

"My seers'll hand out a warming drink to all the raiders before we kick-off. Of course, it'll contain appropriate ingredients to ensure the desired results, including a double dose of Viagra each."

"Sounds great, but how will you focus the blame on Blood-Axe and Olaf? Then, how will you avoid arrest?"

"I'll not be there, silly. From my sick-bed, I'll reluctantly tell 'em to go ahead without me. Believe me, as long as the Konge and Olaf are on the raid, they'll both be in jail or dead by the next day.

"As I instructed her, Aegea has reported the raid to the cops. She doesn't know how much real violence we plan. She's in love with the Konge, so we can't trust her anymore. If all goes to plan, she'll be arrested too."

\*\*\*

A pale carpet of mist hung low over the Great Ouse floodplain around the sleepily awakening village. The streets were deserted except for a barely washed boy delivering the Sunday papers on a bicycle. A couple of early joggers pounded the paths along the riverbank. They gasped "good-days" to an old lady walking her dog when they passed.

As one panted past a spinney he was clubbed from behind and tossed into the slow flowing river. He might have spotted the gathering raiders hiding in the bushes. His body snagged face-down among the reads.

High above, a golden eagle rode a thermal. It relayed pictures into Freyja's quarters in the Seers' Hall. With satisfaction, she pointed to one of the screens.

"Look Ranulf, the police are getting out of their vans and coaches. They're forming up in the playing fields' car park, behind the High Street.

"Great! They're in full riot gear. Fortunately, I passed the wrong time to Aegea. They'll be too late to intervene, but just in time to scoop up Olaf and Blood-Axe."

With his superior eyesight, Ranulf saw something in the corner of the screen.

"What's that?"

She sent a signal on her small control box. The eagle swooped down for a lower pass.

"It's a police drone with a camera. Shit! If it flies that route, they'll see the raiders too early."

Expertly, she pushed the tiny joy-stick forward with her thumb. The eagle dived, crushing the plastic blades of the drone, grasping it in its talons.

In a white police van, the controller saw his view spin. Then the screen went blank.

"Bugger! The drone's crashed Sir."

"Well get it back up again!"

"I can't Sir."

\*\*\*

Olaf Sigtryggson was still raving from his early morning

potion. Followed by twenty priapic, wild-eyed warriors, he charged into the center of the village from a side street. He gave a blood-curdling war cry. Then he swung his battle axe. Crash! It sank deep into the studded door of the Bull and Bear Pub on the High Street. The oak held, until his third blow splintered it asunder.

Seeking the source of the commotion, the landlady emerged into the bar, bleary-eyed from cooking breakfast for a couple who had rented a room.

"What the fuck's going on?"

She shrank back towards the kitchen as the maddened warriors burst into the bar. One smashed the CCTV camera near the ceiling with a spear thrust. Others started passing out bottles of spirits into eager hands. Some pushed their way through the kitchen door. They threw her roughly down, spreading her across the table. She screamed as they ripped her clothes off

\*\*\*

Wary of Freyja's potions, Aegea and Blood-Axe accepted the proffered drink but pretending to drink, left it untouched. Aegea was alarmed both by Freyja's absence and the obvious blood-lust of some of the men. The shield-maidens were egging them on.

Blood-Axe looked worried. He gripped Aegea's arm.

"We need to stop this right away."

He turned to the nearest shield-maidens, the other three in his body guard.

"I'm calling this raid off."

It was as far as he got. A brawny woman whacked him on the back of his helmet with an axe. He was out cold. Aegea screamed and stepped over his body, brandishing her sword protectively. The other guards simply ran off to join the warriors. They were already torching some of the thatched roofs in the High Street. Flames were roaring up the bundles of tinder-dry reeds.

Aegea tried to revive the Konge. Gently removing the dented war helmet, she was relieved to see his head was un-bloodied, but felt a large lump.

"I'd best get you out of here love."

Leaving the helmet, sword and shield where they lay, she hefted him over her shoulder in a fireman's lift. She staggered away along a nearby road. Waving down a passing motorist, she persuaded the driver to take them to the emergency room at Milton Keynes Hospital.

\*\*\*

In Olney Church Manse, the vicar was pouring milk over her muesli in the kitchen. She heard a commotion and screaming from the town. Looking through her stone mullioned window, she saw towering flames and people running, terrified, from their houses. Vikings were cutting them down before her unbelieving eyes.

Without hesitation she unlocked the connecting door into the church and ran to the bell tower. She swung hard on a bell rope. Clang! Clang! Clang! As the bell swung high it lifted her into the air.

She heard a mighty bang from the main door to the church. Dashing towards the altar, she looked back down the nave. A nightmare vision stood before her.

There was the massive figure of Solveig, in full battle armor. He held a sword dripping with blood. His crazed eyes bulged red. There was no missing the huge swelling in his crotch. He advanced towards her, tossing his shield and sword aside. He started to unbuckle his belt. She cried out.

\*\*\*

In a rush, as their timetable was trashed, the police formed a line across the top half of the High Street. Advancing behind their Perspex riot shields, they moved slowly forward in step. Yelling and roaring Vikings were burning, raping and looting right in front of them. The police emerged from the smoke. One of the shield-maidens yelled,

"Shield-wall! Shield-wall!"

As the police line approached behind their Perspex shields, a double row of Vikings locked their round wooden shields to meet them with a clatter of wood on wood. The police line lasted only moments as, yelling the war cry "Blood-Axe!" the Vikings smashed down riot shields with axes and swords. The police broke and ran, leaving their dead and wounded behind them.

\*\*\*

The next day Freyja sat on the sofa in a safe-house with Ranulf. They were watching the BBC news.

A helicopter relayed the scenes around Olney. A pall of dust and smoke still hung over the area. You could see burnt-out houses. The fire-brigade was still hosing the smoldering church. Its roof had collapsed into the nave. The spire had fallen. There were gaps in the High Street where houses once stood. The presenter sounded serious.

"The full horror of murder, arson and rape that took place

in this peaceful English village is still being revealed. Thirty-two bodies have been found so far. Seven are those of policemen. Fifty-four people are being treated in hospitals in Milton Keynes and Northampton. Eight are in critical condition."

The studio presenter burst into the transmission.

"We are interrupting this broadcast to take you to Downing Street, where the Prime Minister is about to make a statement. There will be flash photography."

The camera showed the microphone outside the Prime Minister's official residence at Number 10. The grim-faced Premier stepped though the Georgian door and up to the microphone. Her Home Secretary stood at one side and the Metropolitan Police Commissioner on the other.

"Our hearts go out to those who have suffered loss and injuries at the hands of these murderous terrorists. Everything possible is being done to take care of the injured. His Majesty the King will be visiting the hospitals later today."

Cameras flashed. The media crowded in front of her, thrusting their microphones forward.

She continued in her fake sincere and caring tone.

"My government has declared a state of emergency. We have proscribed the Vikings as a terrorist organization. Their websites praise every act of robbery, violence, and debauchery as deeds of manliness. All their websites have been closed down and any members still at large are asked to give themselves up to the police. I will now hand over to Police Commissioner Gwyneth Davies, to update you on the ongoing investigation."

The butch-haired woman in her mannish uniform stepped forward and spoke in a confident voice.

"We've already, arrested the so-called King of the Vikings, Sir Christopher Walls. He was captured as he attempted to leave Milton Keynes hospital with minor injuries earlier this morning. He has been moved to Paddington Green police station in London under armed guard. He is being questioned under caution. Charges are expected soon. There have been fifty-eight other arrests. Raids have taken place on premises at Viking bases around the area of Newport Pagnell, in Buckinghamshire. There are Police road blocks on the M1 and other major roads in and around Northampton, Bedford and Milton Keynes. We ask the public to stay calm and to accept the major traffic problems that have resulted."

# CHAPTER 10

## TRIALS AND TRIBULATIONS

*"There is no harsher tyranny, than that conducted under the shield of law and the name of justice"*

Charles de Montesquieu

S ir Christopher Walls, aka Blood-Axe, slumped, battered and bruised, handcuffed to a steel chair. It was bolted to an interview room floor in London's Paddington Green Police Station. His head still throbbed. He was puzzled by what had happened to him. He was piecing together what he knew. Freyja must have done all this, the evil horror.

His lawyer was discussing his situation. Blood-Axe sensed that the police waited outside, impatient to resume their interrogation.

"Well Sir Christopher, they've charged you with conspiracy to commit acts of terrorism and accessory to murder, rape and arson. I understand that you are a person of interest in several disappearances, especially that of retired Air Vice Marshal Michael Jackson. They say there are likely to be many more charges later."

Chris looked gloomily up from the table.

"I keep telling everyone—One day, I'm running a successful entertainment organization, getting knighted and all is well. Next, I'm battered and chained to this damned steel chair."

"Yes, well it would be a good idea not to tell anyone anything else. You've said too much without legal advice already.

"As you know, they have forensic evidence from your helmet, equipment and sword found at the scene. They see you as the main perpetrator in all this. Therefore, there's no point in trying to cut a deal by testifying against the others. You could get a marginally lighter sentence by pleading guilty and avoiding the expense of a trial. I doubt it though. The prosecution seems keen on the publicity a successful trial will bring. The Home office is determined to make an example of you."

Chris put his head in his hands for a minute, trying to clear his throbbing brain. Then he moaned.

"But I was drugged and framed by Freyja. It was a set-up."

"That may all be true, but no jury is likely to believe it. Besides, this Freyja has disappeared, along with the friend you call Olaf. Meanwhile, there are lots of Vikings selling you out in return for lighter sentences."

Chris let himself sink back into despair.

***

In New Scotland Yard, in his smartest uniform, Detective Chief Superintendent Masher faced the panel of senior investigating police officers. A grey-haired, grey-suited Home Office observer sat quietly in the background, noting salient points on his iPad.

Masher had already been suspended for three weeks after the Olney incident. He knew his career was over. He gave his account of how he was misinformed about the timing of the incident. He was asked to wait outside.

The Home Office Mandarin remarked.

"Look. No doubt he was incompetent and kept things too much to himself, but we need to divert blame away from the police in all this. It's up to you to follow the correct procedure, of course. All I want to ensure is that you understand the government would much prefer it if he were allowed to retire quietly; after he signs the appropriate disclaimers and documents of course."

The Chairman of the panel, a retired Chief Constable, added a comment.

"The most embarrassing thing of all is the role of Detective Constable O'Malley, aka Aegea. She was clearly complicit in much of the goings on whilst undercover. Masher obviously knew all about it. If she gives evidence in court it'll cause a major public scandal."

Police Commissioner Davies looked around at her fellow officers, asserting her position as highest-ranking police officer in England.

"That's right. She can't give evidence. If she signs a statement saying she acted beyond her instructions in exchange for immunity we can hush the whole thing up. That is if nothing leaks from this room."

She gave a meaningful look around her colleagues.

\*\*\*

A week later, Commissioner Davies called newly retired Dirk Masher. He gripped the phone tightly, furious at the sound of her voice. She tried to sound friendly. He bristled.

"Look, Dirk I know we've had our differences, but we need to talk."

"You've got a damned cheek. You got me the sack."

"Actually Dirk, I protected you from a conspiracy charge and jail. Hear me out.

"The reason I'm calling, is I have a special mission for you. We'll pay you an attractive consultancy fee, but it's hush-hush and you'll report privately to me."

"OK, you've got my attention. Keep talking."

"You know O'Malley better than any of us Dirk. Since the trial, MI5 have had her under full observation and she's been playing by the rules. She's paid a number of visits to Chris Walls in Belmarsh Prison. She can do that, as a private citizen. Of course, we monitor the visits closely. Again, there's nothing to worry about, so far.

"I want you to establish unofficial contact with her. See what you can find out. None of us were happy when that Freyja woman managed to wriggle off the hook and retrieve the rights to Viking assets. The Prime Minister is livid. Still, it's water under the bridge. Freyja and the one they call Olaf must be feeling pretty smug. We'll get them in the end of course.

"I want to know at the first whiff of any contact between the Vikings outside and those inside. Understand?"

"Mmm. Let's discuss the money. I'll also want immunity from prosecution."

"I can arrange that too Dirk."

***

At his Old Bailey trial, a few months earlier, Sir Christopher Walls was persuaded to plead guilty to conspiracy to commit various crimes in exchange for the Crown not proceeding with other charges. This limited anti-government publicity.

Bewigged Lord Justice Rasp looked down his nose over his half-glasses at the sentencing. He noted the armed police standing around the rear of the court. Chris Walls looked warily about him. He stood small and insignificant behind the armored glass of the dock, between two burly guards in body armor.

Looking grimly at Chris, the judge gave his sentence.

"Christopher Walls, you have been found guilty of conspiracy on some of the most heinous crimes ever to be brought before this court. Your evil deeds have led to life sentences of loss and suffering for all those widows, children and relatives of the bereaved and the others who suffered torture, disablement and rape. Nothing can ever repair the damage that you did.

"I therefore sentence you to life imprisonment. There will be no parole for at least thirty years. Take him down."

Chris's mind reeled. Thirty Years. No Parole. I'll be dead in ten. As Chris shuffled off to the cells, head hanging low, to await transport to maximum security prison, relatives of the bereaved screamed abuse and anger from the gallery.

In his chambers, the judge took sherry with the opposing

barristers. They chinked glasses and smiled. It was a job well done. Justice was served.

# CHAPTER 11

## DRAMA AT BELMARSH

*Just Living is not enough. One needs
sunshine, freedom and a little flower.*

Hans Christian Anderson

That Tuesday at Belmarsh maximum security prison in London began like every other routine day. The more relaxed approach was to allow them to mix freely. It was due to the Governor and Home Office caving in to pressure from human rights groups and Chris's supporters outside. It was 7:00 am. The guards rousted out the prisoners from their cells.

"Come on you lot. Let's be 'avin yer. Get in line. If youse want feedin' yer'd best get a move on."

As the sleepy-eyed convicts emerged, they were chivvied into the queue. The screws escorted them along the corridors to the showers and thence to the canteen. Some of the Vikings gave knowing looks to their comrades as they shuffled along. This was routine for the guards, but as they were managing convicted terrorists, they tried to stay alert.

Prisoner 683947 Sir Christopher Walls, aka Konge Blood-Axe, had been moved from the Isolation Wing following demonstrations and a campaign organized by Amnesty International. Now, he was on the same wing as most of his ex-Viking comrades. Some of them were already soaping themselves in the showers.

Blood-Axe expected anything but a routine day. He stayed back in his cell. When the warders came to chase him out, he lay on his bunk, groaning loudly. Suspecting malingering, a tall warder with a broken nose and dark hair showing beneath his cap stepped towards him.

"Come on, we're 'avin none o' that. Git yerself up now."

Blood-Axe vomited over the man's uniformed trousers and shoes. The screw leapt back in disgust.

Summoned over the radio, a medic rushed into the room. The prisoner's blood pressure was up and his temperature soaring.

"Fetch a gurney down here. We need to get the prisoner to the hospital wing pronto."

Blood-Axe wretched and moaned. He began gasping for breath. This spurred them on as they wheeled him off down the white corridor towards the elevator. Before he reached the prison hospital, the Governor and Prison Doctor were notified. The smuggled pills had worked their magic.

\*\*\*

Freyja emerged from hiding when the charges against her were dropped. She hired a top law firm to recover most of the Viking assets.

In the past month she had become increasingly frustrated. She had hoped that, with the Konge in prison, her accession to the remaining trappings of Viking power would be a foregone conclusion. Several events thwarted her plans.

She recalled the worrying dispatch from her top agent in Moscow.

*"CIA Viking member Ivan Vasilov has been caught in a clumsy plot. He tried to replace the Jarl of the local chapter here. The SVR (the foreign intelligence arm of the Russian Federation), has tracked the whole US Viking membership from the start. In close cooperation with their comrades in the FSB (the counter intelligence arm of Russian state security), they have infiltrated our Russian Vikings. Russian authorities have triggered an internal bloodbath,*

*resulting in the deaths of twenty-four CIA agents and assets around the world."*

Due to this, Langley was using the NSA to jam global Viking communications and there had been mass arrests in the US. Other nations' security services were also investigating the perceived CIA infiltration of the Vikings.

As if this was not bad enough, there was dissent in what was left of the Viking Council. It was developing as a reaction to the domination of the male Vikings by Freyja's shield-maidens and was becoming a direct challenge to her leadership.

***

Sysselman John Chandler, ex-stockbroker and Guards officer, now known as Olaf Sigtryggson, had hatched a plot to have Freyja assassinated from his own safe house somewhere in Ireland. He escaped the debacle in Olney because his henchmen had spirited him away before the police could nab him. Later, old-Harrovian chums in the Home Office ensured that charges against him were dropped due to procedural errors and contaminated forensics.

\*\*\*

It was a moonless night. Three men dressed in black and wearing balaclavas crept towards Freyja's private quarters. Their stealthy footsteps were masked by her screams of ecstasy, as Ranulf thrust into her. When her door burst open, she was at the point of no return. She let out a giant moan of frustration when Ranulf rolled out of her.

An assassin stabbed a dagger between Ranulf's shoulders. To the man's dismay, the blade snapped clean off. Ranulf back-fisted the side of his assailant's head, pulping his brain. Seemingly impervious to other knife thrusts, Ranulf grasped one man's wrist and with his other hand, wrenched at his torso, roaring with rage. With a crunching sound the arm was torn clean off. The last man fled into the darkness with a broken arm, the shrieks of his dismembered comrade echoing in his ears.

As a result of that incident and the general mood, Freyja was forced to reach an accommodation with Olaf Sigtryggson. They were to rule jointly. The Viking Council demanded that they spring Blood-Axe from Belmarsh. She went along with the planning, but had ideas of her own as to whether the attempt should succeed.

\*\*\*

"Take 21." The clapperboard snapped yet again. The cameras rolled. In a disused gravel-pit just off the M3 motorway South West of London, a pitched battle was underway. It was obviously part of a movie shoot. This was the eighth rehearsal.

It was a WWII movie about the Russian Army. Viking Olaf Sigtryggson bellowed instructions at his men through a megaphone. They were running about wearing antique Soviet Army uniforms.

He had always liked dressing up. When in the British Army he had loved strutting about in his red guard's officer's coat and tall black bearskin hat. At the annual trooping of the colour, he paraded his men, glittering dress-sword in hand. He got a thrill from marching up and down. He always felt a mystic power as he roared "Eyes right!" to his company; their heads snapping round in unison towards the Sovereign reviewing the parade on his horse.

This Soviet general's uniform was quite swanky too. The unfamiliar high and round flat top of the olive-green peaked hat and golden shoulder boards were a novelty. He was amused by the Soviet style of wearing large medals plastered all over the front of his tunic. NATO forces sported neat rows of smaller medals. Americans wore three times as many as Brits.

He chuckled to himself that the unearned medals, Gold Star Hero of the Soviet Union, Order of the Red Banner, and Order of Lenin, were as valid as the many non-combat-medals awarded for good conduct or performance in various tasks by US and NATO forces.

In WW II the Russians had driven back the Germans with massive casualties on both sides and no quarter given. Maybe they had won World War II, and not the Americans. Their twenty-million war dead supported that theory.

This filming idea was a terrific wheeze. It allowed the carrying of some pretty effective hardware without arousing suspicion. Firing off all these blanks and flash bangs was a lot better than dodging Afghan bullets too.

A few rustics watched the comings and goings of the T34-85 tanks, six-wheeled trucks and the brown uniforms of the men as they traipsed into the quarry each day and emerged later covered in grime and mud. As intended, the locals paid less attention to them over time.

Olaf's men grumbled during their tea break. They were Vikings not Communists.

"This uniform's making me itch. It's all scratchy and uncomfortable. They had crap fabric in Russia."

"What's the point of all this? Besides it's raining. I'm getting piss wet."

They grumbled. Was it some elaborate entertainment for Olaf's stuck up friends? Why should they have to do this? One of the platoon leaders, dressed as a Soviet Commissar, sporting a red star on his grey fake-fur hat, grunted.

"Stop whining, for fuck's sake. How often do you get to play with all these antique weapons and explosives? I'm havin' a great time. All this vodka warms me up as well."

\*\*\*

Juliette O'Malley, aka Aegea, had no contact with Freyja after Blood-Axe's incarceration. She was pleased about this. Her love for the Konge had only strengthened during her prison visits. He was a fascinating man. As she got to know him better, and in his current hardship, she could see that he only ever wanted to make his people happy, rather than to cause pain and suffering. What happened to him was unfair. Freyja was clearly still a threat to him.

O'Malley hated to view Blood-Axe through the bullet-proof glass in the prison visiting booth. She assumed that transcripts of every word they spoke were relayed to the Governor and the police.

Her hopes were raised when Olaf's, agents approached her. She was astonished and suspicious to learn that he had formed a coalition with Freyja. They wanted O'Malley to rejoin them. She was reluctant, but it seemed like the Konge's only hope. They brought her into planning for the breakout from Belmarsh. She was a trusted source for Blood-Axe and they could use her as a go-between to the Konge.

\*\*\*

Since the assassination attempt on Freyja, the towering figure of Ranulf never left her side. His eyes and ears seemed to miss nothing as Freyja gave Aegea her orders.

"Your role is to get a message to the Konge about our plan. The prison is equipped with the latest anti-drone defenses. We circumvent these using the jackdaws. Their brains are controlled with technology perfected in my secret laboratory. An implanted chip manages their missions, whilst to outsiders they looked like a perfectly normal flock of birds.

"The images you see on the screen are from their earlier surveillance flights. The routines and layouts of the prison are well understood. The next mission will be for one of the jackdaws to die in a corner of the exercise yard. A trusted prisoner will remove a pill and a message from its gut. They will be passed to the Kong. Ensure that he expects that message, without the eavesdroppers being alerted. Understood?"

She understood well enough but had no trust in Freyja. On the other hand, Olaf seemed a genuine friend to Blood-Axe. He plotted with her when Freyja was not present to arrange diversions. These would keep her erstwhile police colleagues well away from the rescue attempt.

\*\*\*

Dirk Masher looked around the coffee addicts in the

London Piccadilly branch of an international chain. He never understood why some liked cream, candies and sickly-sweet sauces piled high on their coffee. Maybe they hated the taste of coffee? His eyes cast about the noisy room for former detective Constable O'Malley, aka Aegea.

He grudgingly conceded that O'Malley knew how to choose a discrete venue. He had requested this face-to-face meeting when she had revealed a new major Viking plot. She was fearful of being followed and had suggested this place.

Poorly cleaned tables and scruffy easy chairs accommodated gaggles of chattering office workers. There was a long line waiting to order their daily caffeine fixes. Others hung around the counter waiting for their orders. Some shouted to be heard above the din. Many tapped texts and tweets into their phones. Tourists took selfies of themselves in the queue. *Whatever happened to a leisurely cup of coffee? Who gives a fuck where Mrs. Watanabe from Tokyo gets her carrot cake?*

Spotting O'Malley at a quiet table to the rear, Masher maneuvered his way over, easing his bulk into a wooden chair opposite her. O'Malley pushed a cappuccino she had bought for him across the table. He sipped it, screwing up his face. It wasn't the best in London. He spoke quietly so as not to attract attention.

"Look I know it's difficult for you to meet me in person, but I have to be sure we don't set a lot of hares running and deploy half the anti-terrorist assets in London on a wild goose chase. Since you got me fired, I can't afford any more mistakes."

O'Malley fidgeted nervously. It was part of her act.

"They're going to know it was me. I'll need a false passport and 400,000 pounds. A third in Euros, a third in US dollars and the rest in Sterling; all in untraceable notes."

"You've got to be kidding O'Malley. There's no way they'll do that for a disgraced ex-officer. Besides, they'll protect you."

"Look, I'm sorry, but unless you get me the funds, I'll not share the date of the event with you. The government can afford it. They find money to fight distant wars whenever they need it."

Masher's eyes went to slits. He spluttered and was about to erupt, then remembered they were in a public place. She had a point too. He muttered,

"OK, I'll see what I can do. But you could live to regret this. You know what stingy bastards they are when not feathering their own nests."

\*\*\*

The day before O'Malley met Masher in the coffee bar, she had visited Freyja in her secret quarters. Only three people were present. Freyja calmly issued her instructions to an increasingly incredulous O'Malley. Ranulf stood impassively watching the exchange between the two women.

"Here's your mission. I need you to betray the breakout plan to your friends in the Police. Do it as fast as you can and hide the source if at all possible."

"Please help me to understand. You want me to betray Konge Blood-Axe's escape plan with the other Vikings to the UK authorities?"

"Exactly! I intend to rule here. It's time to remove those who think otherwise. Do you have any problem with that?"

 As Ranulf watched Aegea intently, his hand slid menacingly to the hilt of his short-sword. Aegea broke into a sweat. Seeing that agreement was her only option, she dissembled rapidly. She forced herself to look calm and obedient despite the pounding of her heart.

"No, my Queen. But I'll need protection and some funds to hide for a few weeks afterwards. Can I draw some money and recruit ten warriors to protect me?"

Preening at the idea of her finally becoming Queen, Freyja gave her assent with a regal wave. It felt good, really good.

Back in her lonely bedroom, O'Malley frantically evaluated her limited options. All seemed perilous and required betrayal. If she sold Freyja out to Olaf, the leader of the planned prison escape, Freyja might prevail. Ranulf seemed invincible and the shield-maidens were still a formidable force. Freyja may have other means of tipping off the authorities about the planned escape. In which case, both O'Malley and Blood-Axe would be finished.

If she went along with Freyja's order to blow the secrecy of the breakout, she would be betraying Blood-Axe, the man she now loved. Her fealty to the police was long gone but she would be on the right side of the UK authorities.

Possible problems were many. Olaf could discover the betrayal and seek revenge. Freyja could have her killed anyway, just to cover up her own treachery. If Blood-Axe survived, he would hate her and might seek revenge. She couldn't bear that.

She needed to think of a way out for both her and

Blood-Axe. Little else mattered. At least she could draw some funds and recruit ten warriors loyal to Blood-Axe to support any chosen plan.

\*\*\*

Masher understood the need for secrecy without any urging from O'Malley. He knew that elements of the military, clandestine services and police were still riddled with Viking informers and sympathizers. The recent disasters at the CIA had conclusively proved that.

He conferred with Commissioner Gwyneth Davies. Davies decided to assemble her strike forces at Northolt RAF base, west of London, but to keep the ultimate target to herself. The 22$^{nd}$ SAS Regiment, the Police Anti-terrorist squad and the RAF helicopter forces needed to transport them received only this message.

**"All units need to be on standby at one hour's notice to defend an important target in greater London. You have all prepared for a number of such locations in many exercises. These include airports, barracks, weapons depots, centers of government, prisons, communications hubs,**

**power stations and military control centers.**

**Your top-secret sealed orders will be handed to you in a timely manner.**

**This is not a drill. Ensure that your forces and equipment are ready and act as ordered. The future of the UK may depend on your success."**

When Freyja heard of the assembling forces at RAF Northholt she allowed herself a cold smile, feeling secure in her route to power.

***

Not an hour after Blood-Axe was moved to the hospital wing, the Viking prisoners rioted. Knives, spears and other weapons, fabricated in the prison workshops miraculously appeared. Guards were lying dead. The recreation area was in flames. The London Fire Brigade and the Thames Valley Police were attending.

As the reports started to come in to Northolt RAF base, Commissioner Davies thought to herself, *Aha, the expected diversions have begun.* She picked up the radio and instructed that the sealed orders be handed out. Ten minutes later helicopters were clattering off to the location of their defensive mission.

Whenever Davies glanced at the CCTV images of Belmarsh over the next hour, the fire brigade seemed to be controlling the fire. The Police were keeping the perimeter secure. Radio communications were down but she saw this as all part of a clever diversion.

An innocuous and rather grubby three-ton truck stood, apparently abandoned, in a side street a few hundred yards from Belmarsh. It was crammed with radio jamming and communications equipment. Inside, technicians replayed and rerouted an earlier video recording of the fire brigade and police into the CCTV feed to Northolt, masking the current reality of the situation around the prison.

\*\*\*

The police and fire brigade were under attack. Within minutes they were swept aside in a hail of bullets and the booming of 85mm cannon fire. A large force dressed as World War II Russian Infantry, supported by five late model T34 tanks, was charging through the wreckage of the prison gates. Crushed and burning squad cars and fire engines lay all around.

Shaped demolition charges breached the walls in multiple places. Inmates were swarming out through the gaps. Well used, white Ford Transit vans, like those driven by nearly every tradesman in London, collected them. The vans' crews handed out Kalashnikovs, grenades and Soviet-era PPSh-41 submachine guns with their distinctive drum-fed magazines. The Transits sped off in all directions, dispersing their escaping and now heavily armed prisoners across London to spread further chaos.

Dashing through the smoke and dust of a breach in the wall, Olaf led a crack commando team of his own bodyguards toward the prison hospital. Another group had already secured the Governor and his command center.

A burly Viking dressed as a Russian sergeant blew the hospital door off its hinges with a plastic explosive charge.

Despite their earplugs, half-deafened by the blast, the assault group stepped warily into the ward through the smoke, pointing their guns around the room. They had expected to be greeted by their Konge. Instead, they found doctors and staff in white coats sprawled about the floor, unconscious. The Konge was gone. By the time the intruders smelt gas, it was too late. Olaf's vision was dimming, as he crumpled to the floor. He glimpsed the hole in the back wall of the room. *Oh bugger!* O'Malley had made her own escape plans for the Konge. He'd been played.

***

An Old Norwegian trawler, the Havguden (sea god), slowly churned through a heavy sea to its rendezvous with a forty-foot sailing yacht off the cost of Stavanger, southwest Norway. Both crews scanned their radars, the horizon and the skies, before bringing their craft alongside each other. A sea-sick Blood-Axe, pale and covered in vomit, was swathed in yellow oilskins. He was bundled across to the yacht and down into its cabin. Waiting for him and shoving a whiskey flask towards him was his nephew, Joe, aka Troels the Berserker.

"Drink this Lord. It'll put new heart in you."

Blood-Axe took a deep pull on the flask. He gasped as the fiery liquid seared into his throat and stomach. Looking around at Aegea, Joe and his other stalwart and loyal rescuers he belched and gave them a warm smile. *Maybe we've really got away with it.*

\*\*\*

Back in the UK there had been chaos in the aftermath of the escape. The SAS and the anti-terrorist squad had deployed erroneously in and around the British Parliament buildings. A small diversionary explosion under Westminster Bridge had added to the panic there. In Northholt, Commissioner Davies was screaming at these forces over the radio, trying to retrieve the situation.

"Get over to Belmarsh!

"We were conned! We picked the wrong target.

"Never mind how. Just get there!"

Police helicopters and RAF aircraft were scrambling, trying to track the multiple vehicles fleeing from Belmarsh. All ports and airports were closed. Public transport was shut down. Traffic in and around London was gridlocked by the chaos.

The Prime Minister was beyond furious. The media was baying for blood. She would try to make certain it was not going to be hers. She could not see how though.

At Belmarsh Prison, the surviving Thames Valley

Police had arrested a comatose Olaf and a few of his shock troops. Fleeing from the area, the remaining actors had abandoned their T34 tanks and Soviet uniforms to merge into the puzzled throng trying to get home from London amidst the endless delays.

\*\*\*

Freyja too was frantically seeking the whereabouts of the Konge, with little success. She ordered Ranulf to be ready to leave as soon as he was located.

# CHAPTER 12

## THE CAVE

*"I am in that temper, that if I were under water I would scarcely kick to come to the surface"*

John Keats

Jokelfjord lies far across the North Sea from the UK; high above the Arctic Circle in Norway. Few intrepid adventurers ever visit there, and then mainly in summer. The national park has the largest glacier in Europe and a 6,800-foot mountain. It attracts most of the hardy cross-country skiers and climbers.

In a remote part of the mostly iced-up fjord, shivering between rocky and icy cliffs, in the perpetual winter darkness, lies the entrance to a deep cave. Far inside, the remnants of Blood-Axe's once huge Viking following sat on animal firs. They huddled around the fire for warmth, drank way too much and yarned of previous glories. For Aegea, this seemed the happiest time of her life. What more could she want, than feeling the warmth of the man she loved wrapped within the same huge bear skin.

Blood-Axe hated the place. When they were in their private space, curtained off by Reindeer furs, he confided in her.
"We've got to get out of here. It's too cold, too dark and too bloody boring. The foods tedious and I've had enough."

From beneath his arm, Aegea looked up sadly at him in the flickering candlelight.

"It's not safe outside. We're hunted fugitives. Freyja wants you dead. Besides, where can we go?"

"Well, maybe we'd be better off dead?"

"Don't say that Chris, my love. At least we have each other."

He said," I have an idea. There is only one way this can end, my darling. We need to make it happen."

***

Freyja was also keeping a low profile. Her greatest fears had come to pass. The Belmarsh debacle resulted in the Vikings being once again a proscribed terrorist organization. Almost all of the money, her money as she saw it, had been seized by the authorities. She was down to her last hundred million dollars. Unlike Blood-Axe, her bolt-hole was rather more commodious.

She had totally changed her appearance, of course. Gone were the witchy black hair, the piercings and all the rest. Now she was a suntanned blond, stretching herself on a sun lounger by the sixty-foot pool of her Marbella Villa in sunny Spain.

Ranulf was rubbing oil into her back with powerful strokes of his huge, firm hands. She purred at his every touch. After a while she told him, "Enough!" She propped herself up on an elbow and re-read the message on her tablet for a second time, this time out loud.

"I've heard that those idiots are somewhere in Norway. Here's the message that came encrypted on the Darknet."

**"To all loyal Vikings: Our saga is approaching its end. Your Konge, Blood-Axe, is diagnosed with incurable cancer. He is preparing to meet the gods. Gather in Nordfjordat midsummer to do him honor."**

She clicked on Google Maps, pointing at the screen.

"Look it's the middle of nowhere. No wonder we couldn't find the sniveling swine."

She sneered.

"He must have had a miserable time up there, freezing his balls off."

Ranulf looked impassively at her.

"Shall we prepare to attend this event my Queen?"

"No, stupid. Why should he be allowed any kind of glorious send-off? You are to go and kill him as soon as possible. His body must never be found."

Freyja turned on the UK TV news with the remote.

"Breaking news—The body of a middle-aged woman has been found floating in Ullswater in the lake district. A source close to the local police says it is that of Police Commissioner Gwyneth Davies. She went missing from her home after the Belmarsh Prison escape a few weeks ago. We understand that foul play is not suspected."

Freyja crowed with delight, punching a fist in the air.

"So, the useless cow decided to end it all. Another victory for the Vikings."

\*\*\*

In his Norwegian cave, Blood-Axe's diminished band was feasting on reindeer meat, fish, whiskey and blood sausage. A pile of automatic firearms and other weapons lay at the back of the cave.

Blood-Axe's nephew, Troels the Berserker, was reading

his favorite story, the **Haraldskvæði saga,** from a leather-bound volume. **His now deep-bass voice reverberated around the cavern.**

"I will enquire of the berserker, you drinkers of blood,
Those fearless heroes, how are you treated,
Those who stride out into battle?
Wolf-skinned you are called. In battle
They heft bloody shields.
Red with gore are their spears.

When they advance to fight,
They form a tight cluster.
The wise king trusts such men,
Who hack through enemy shields."

The others glanced at each other. Troels fitted the image. During the raid on Olney, he had been seen chewing on a still beating heart, torn from a man's chest with his bare hands. He'd also been observed chomping on the upper rim of his shield. Now, in a restful mood, he was his usual mild-mannered self. However, they all noticed the distant fire burning in his eyes as he ended the recital with great passion.

Following the reading, they sat in silence, staring into the peat-fire flame, savoring the crescendos and resonances of the tale. Their hearts were inspired, remembering the thrill of being the Vikings they once were. The smoke curled and billowed up through a great crack in the roof of the cave, high above.

Troels raised the issue of the invitation that the Konge had sent forth. It was done against his advice and the warnings of all the others. However, he was still their Konge, even in the cold isolation of this adversity.

\*\*\*

Next morning, Troels arrived breathless from a hike down to the nearby hamlet.

"My Konge—A friendly neighbor reports that strangers are appearing in some of the villages and holiday resorts around the fjord. We need to be alert. They may be hostile. Perhaps the authorities are on to us?"

"You're right Troels. Check the Claymore mines on all the approaches. Ensure all the weapons are oiled and let's post guards."

Blood-Axe recalled the training that Olaf had brought to them from his days in the Grenadier Guards. Claymores are high-explosive mines pegged into the ground. Each could spray lethal shrapnel in a semicircle. Triggered by a trip wire or a remote signal they could easily protect the few rocky and very steep trails leading to their eyrie, halfway up a cliff.

\*\*\*

A white-tailed eagle soared on its eight-foot-wide, barn-door wings, high above the fjord, seeing everything below. Spotting a large fish beneath the surface, it folded its brown wings, hurtling down. As it streaked low over the smooth surface of the water it dipped its yellow talons under the surface. It seized its prey, dragging the silver, wildly struggling sea-trout into the air. As the large fish struggled, the eagle made small corrections in its flight with its signature white, fanned tail. It flapped away to the top of a dead tree. There it devoured its meal, tearing it asunder with its powerful yellow, hooked bill.

Two pairs of eyes observed this display of aerobatic skill. Hidden among some dried bracken, Troels the Berserker was entranced. He watched the whole event through his binoculars. It was a brief and welcome distraction from the tedious vigil of guarding the trails and surroundings of the cave.

From the shade afforded by some rocks across the fjord, Ranulf needed no binos. Thanks to the Cranfield Laboratory, his brain was attuned directly to the eagle's. As the bird identified the fish, it had also traced the lightly used paths. Ranulf noticed a bent twig here, a footmark on a patch of lichen there. He noted the locations of the Claymore mines, trip wires and their laser triggers. He was especially pleased to identify

Troels' hiding place as the berserker's attention was glued to the bird.

\*\*\*

As mid-summer approached, the hours of daylight lengthened. In the few hours of darkness, Ranulf stealthily swam across the fjord. The water was close to freezing as it ran off the glacier but he seemed impervious to the chill, wearing only deerskins for ease of movement. Taking infinite care, he silently picked his way up between rocks. Finally, he approached the cave mouth. With super-human senses, he identified and avoided the lasers and tripwires meant to alert those inside and trigger the Claymore mines.

The cave-mouth guard thought he heard a leaf rustle. He looked to his right. Ranulf seized his head from behind and wrenched it round. His neck cracked as his spinal column snapped. The intruder softly let the body down to the ground.

Silently pushing aside the leather door cover, he entered the cave. He dispatched two sleeping Vikings with his knife before the alarm was raised. The next man gave a blood-curdling scream before his throat was slashed. It ended in a bubbling, bloody gurgle.

The others jumped into action. Seizing a battle-axe,
Troels roared with rage. Seeing Ranulf's bloodied hands,
his eyes rolled and he began to foam with fury. He
charged forward. Ranulf raised his short-sword in the
confined space. With one massive blow he calmly
slashed off Troels' hand.

Bellowing with pain and anger, Troels hurled himself
forward. Ranulf deftly thrust his blade deep into Joe's
belly. The momentum carried Troels onward. He gouged
at Ranulf's eyes with the last of the failing strength in his
left hand. He bit down hard on his nose. As the light
faded from his eyes, he felt the undamaged metallic
eyeballs and the plastic skin pulling away from Ranulf's
face.

Ranulf tossed the body aside with one arm. He advanced
on Blood-Axe. The Konge was coming forward,
desperately manipulating a short, olive-green cylinder he
had grabbed from the weapons pile. Acgea ran between
them preparing for her last fight. She yelled,

"No!"

Distracted momentarily, Ranulf raised his sword arm to
slash down on her head.

The Konge yelled,

"Get down!"

Instinctively, she ducked to avoid the sweep of the

sword. A flash of searing heat singed her hair. Blood-Axe had triggered the LAW (Light Anti-Tank Weapon) from its extendable plastic tube. The explosive charge blew Ranulf's head to pieces, hurling his body backwards. The blast and the back-flash of the rocket in the confined space stunned them all. It sucked the air from their lungs.

Ranulf's corpse lay on the cave floor. Blackened electric wires, projecting from his neck, emitted a few sparks. The stump of a titanium spine projected up to where the cranium should be. It became clear that Ranulf had been a robot.

\*\*\*

The heroic deaths of the Viking leadership made news headlines throughout the world. A Norwegian doctor friendly to the Vikings issued death certificates for the deceased. The autopsy was conducted by another Viking sympathizer.

 The Norwegian Government forbade any public funeral or demonstrations. In the face of protest marches in world capitals and powerful lobbying from its own local community, it relented. It could be a boost for tourism in the region. A Viking long-ship was prepared in the traditional style.

# Chapter 13

## An ending Fit for a Konge

*"It was a fitting end for a heroic life. He, who set the world ablaze, was born away to Valhalla in his flaming long-ship. As the fire burned its timbers to the level of the waves, his soul passed to join the gods, his berserker, his brave enemies and the heroes of ages past.*

*His battles and deeds will live forever. Here on earth the strong timbers of his ship burned to the waves and his ashes were born away by the Valkyrie. Now, he sits at the right hand of Odin and sups with Thor in Valhalla. His saga will be sung forever, wherever Vikings gather."*

The Blood-Axe Saga

Thousands of mourners lined the shore of the fjord. News helicopters circled above.

Paparazzi thronged around one figure who feigned a desire to avoid the limelight. Retired Chief Inspector Masher, his ruddy face made even redder by the blazing torches, "reluctantly" said a few well-rehearsed, self-serving and trite words.

"I got to know Konge Blood-Axe after I nicked him for the Olney massacre. He wasn't a bad sort really. The whole thing just got out of hand. As for the break-out from Belmarsh—that wasn't his doing at all. I always suspected that the Russians were behind it. It took that level of sophistication and planning. Besides where did it get him? A miserable death in a freezing cold place. I'll be revealing many things in my book."

Having ensured that his client had appeared on all the

major news channels, Masher's agent whisked him away. His lucrative book deal was just the start. He was also technical advisor on the first movie on the life and death of Blood-Axe. There was also a full calendar of well-paid public speaking engagements around the world.

Another figure, a woman, watched cold-eyed from behind large dark glasses and a hoodie. Freyja had landed on her feet. The CIA had recruited her to run a robotics and cyborg lab at Los Alamos for its black programs. The agency's high regard for her skills, knowledge and global network of ex-shield-maidens and Valkyries had allowed her to demand attendance at this event.

She was surrounded by four minders at all times. They had orders to shoot to kill if she even looked like she might try and make a break for it. She smiled. She could easily take them, but why would she? She had already built several superior versions of Ranulf. They proved even more satisfying in her bed. She also had unlimited funds available to build armies of robot warriors for the US government. Her day of absolute power was postponed, not cancelled.

She regarded the pantomime funeral with contempt. Who cared about the dead body of a former lover? Blood-Axe had thwarted her plans. *He could have had a minor role under my leadership if he had played his cards right. Instead, he died in this cold and miserable fjord. Silly old fool.* She began to scan the mourners and revelers. Her real purpose at this event was to spot team-members who she could use again in the future.

She nibbled her lip in frustration. She had hoped to see the traitor, Aegea. *That bitch deserves retribution for all the trouble she's caused me. When I find her, she'll get what's coming and it won't be quick.* CIA reports stated that Aegea's body was not in the cave. *So, she's at large somewhere. Oh well, a good manhunt keeps life interesting.*

Standing inches taller than most of the men present, another woman attracted some media interest. Dressed in a fashionable fake fur coat and hat, Lady Drika Walls was holding court and enjoying the clamor of attention. It made a change from her weekly round of book club meetings, church fund-raisers, Zumba, yoga and shopping expeditions. She had attended every day of Blood-Axe's trial, savoring each humiliation and accusation heaped upon him. If he'd listened to her, none of this would have happened. On the other hand, she enjoyed being a minor celebrity. Especially since his spectacular break-out from prison, she was often in the papers. She was even invited to parties by those interested in being seen with well-known people rather than sparkling conversation. Microphones were thrust into her face.

"What was it like being married to Blood-Axe, Drika?"

"Was he a good lover?"

"Why did you leave him?"

"Was he violent?"

A contingent of burly men and tough looking women in Viking costume sang, drank and thronged the jetty. A parade of others from the Shetlands marched down to the dock. They whirled blazing braziers on chains around their heads in fiery circles. They tossed them into the pitch-soaked faggots on the long-ship. Flames illuminated the dragon's head snarling down on the crowd from high above her prow.

The vessel was hastily caste off before the wooden jetty could catch fire. Orange tongues licked her billowing sail and flared up the mast. The imposing figure of the Konge Blood-Axe, laid out in full armor with his war-shield across his chest and sword in hand, flickered in the flames. The burnished cheek-pieces of his battle-helmet reflected the white-hot glow. Fully ablaze now, the lean lines of her hull drifted out to sea on the tide and current.

Finally, the fireball became just a fading gleam on the horizon. The crowd, now utterly silent, watched it disappear. There was a great collective sigh as the waves extinguished the last reflections on the sea.

\*\*\*

In South London, Belmarsh Prison was under reconstruction, to include anti-tank obstacles and enhanced electronic security. The Viking terrorists were held in some of the repaired cells.

Olaf Sigtryggson, aka John Chandler, watched the funeral on the large-screen TV in his cell. He silently applauded the realism of the spectacle. As the leader of the incarcerated and the remnants of the Vikings still at large, he commanded respect and special treatment. He had negotiated a peaceful regime with the new governor. The discussions had reminded him of those in Taliban villages in Afghanistan. There was suspicion on both sides but nobody wanted to die or lose face.

He spent his days on his own book about the events of the Blood-Axe saga. Otherwise, he relieved the tedium with meetings with his literary agent and legal team. He was seeking early parole. His friends in the government, the Army and the Civil Service were making encouraging noises. There was a stream of other visitors. He was quite a celebrity, with substantial daily correspondence. Eventually, he would have to decide which proposal of marriage to accept. Still, there was no rush yet.

\*\*\*

Freyja was ready to leave Blood-Axe's funeral. *At last, this pantomime is over. Damn Blood-Axe to hell! Well at least I beat the bastard. I always come out on top.*

High up on the opposite mountain across the fjord, Aegea was cloaked in darkness. She made a minute adjustment to the sight on her CheyTac M200 sniper rifle. A similar weapon had been used by a Brit to kill an ISIS fighter at a then record range of 2.4 kilometers in Iraq some years earlier. John Chandler, aka Olaf, had supplied this weapon to Aegea a few months earlier.

Freyja's head was lit up by the light of the blazing torches held by some on the jetty. Aegea made a tiny adjustment. The crosshairs centered on her target's brow at 1.53 kilometers. Not an easy shot, but doable. There was very little wind. She calmed her breath. Her heartbeat had increased and she consciously slowed it. She spoke to her companion as she stroked the trigger. He was viewing the target through his spotting scope. He had made the computer calculations for the shot. These took into account their distance, height above the target and wind speeds.

"I have the target. She's ready to leave. Permission to fire?"

He grunted.

"Do it!"

Keeping her whole body steady, ever so gently she squeezed the trigger. There was a sharp crack. The over-pressured .338 Lapua Magnum bullet, as issued to UK special forces, blasted from the barrel at supersonic speed. It would strike before its sound was heard. After the recoil, Aegea had time to adjust her aim, ready for a second shot in case Freyja had moved her head, forcing a miss.

*But no, it's unnecessary.* Freyja's head exploded in a red mist. Her body was hurled backwards. Her CIA protectors snatched out their weapons, snapping their heads around in confusion. They tried to see where the shot came from. Panicking, the crowd ran off in all directions.

Far from their vision, the sniper team calmly walked away. Aegea tossed the weapon off a cliff-top pathway into the fjord far below. They hid for a while, under a thermal aluminum blanket in a hollow. Norwegian military helicopters with infrared sensors clattered overhead. Circling a few times, they registered no body heat and soared away to search elsewhere.

\*\*\*

The last word is best left to the Blood-Axe Saga.

*"So, sing the praises of our dead Konge. Spread his fame. As new generations arise, ensure that they hear of these glorious events. Perhaps in years to come, new Vikings will arise and do great deeds. Until then, Konge Blood-Axe will be remembered as the last of the great Viking Warriors."*

# Epilogue

*"I must learn to be content with being Happier than I deserve."*

Jane Austen


*"And hand in hand on the edge of the sand,*

*They danced by the light of the moon, the moon.*

*They danced by the light of the moon."*

Edward Lear - The Owl and the Pussy Cat

It was yet another incredible sunset in Costa Rica. Through the gently swaying slatted silhouettes of the palms, the red orb of the sun lit the sky across the entire Pacific horizon.

Reflections of fiery clouds and patches of bright blue sky rippled over the gentle ocean waves. The balmy evening air breathed a soft sigh over Mr. and Mrs. McClusky, formerly Blood-Axe and Aegea. They lounged on the patio of their new home, enthralled, as the iridescent hummingbirds sucked their last nectar of the day from the red, sweet-scented hibiscus flowers.

They leaned into each other on a swing seat overlooking their infinity pool. With one arm draped around her shoulder Chris sipped from the gin and tonic in his other hand and gently rocked the swing with his leg. She sighed, tasting her Piña Colada and looked lovingly into his eyes.

"Well we had quite an adventure. Not many let their wild inner Viking loose like we did."

He smiled back.

"It's funny how we were all carried away by the Viking culture. Maybe it was the drugs, or perhaps something in our genes. I still half-believe."

"The gene theory sounds a bit far-fetched Chris. Though, I remember reading that some scientists claim that belief in God could be genetic. This could be the same."

"Whatever. You saved me again my love. Only you could have persuaded the Norwegian doctor and the pathologist to fake my death and substitute an unknown corpse from the morgue.

"Who would have thought we could have such a happy ending? You took my revenge on Freyja as well."

She squeezed his arm.

"I fired at your command my love. It was vengeance for both of us."

They sat, content, hand-in-hand. The last tiny

segment of the blood-red sun dipped below the horizon. Then with a roar like a runaway express train, a massive earthquake shook the house. Some tiles on the patio cracked. The water in the pool sloshed over the sides. The swing rocked violently, spilling their drinks down their T-shirts. Some of the light fittings crashed to the ground. All the lamps flickered and went out.

He shouted as he staggered towards the house. Something from his memory drove his unsteady legs over the quivering ground.

"Stay here!"

She tried to follow, but the next tremor threw her to the floor, bruising her arm. He fell too but seemed desperate to get something. She screamed after him.

"Don't go in! It's dangerous!"

As if to underline her point, part of the roof fell in. Scrambling through the dust and wreckage he was desperate to find his sword. He remembered Freyja's teaching. *Only gripping a weapon, can you get to Valhalla.* A minute later he emerged, wild-eyed, tightly grasping his Viking short-sword. He pulled his new wife up and clasped her to him.

The next tremor was even greater. A gigantic fissure opened in the earth. The house collapsed, tumbling into it. They were thrown down on the remains of the wrecked patio which teetered on the brink of the crevasse. She slipped towards the edge. He seized her arm, holding her dangling. She looked imploringly into his eyes. He started to slip in too as the patio tilted to forty degrees. He held his sword tightly in one hand and her arm in the other. The earth swallowed them. As, they fell into the darkness, he screamed his defiance of the Earth.

"To Valhalla my love!"

# Earlier Vikings

Apologists for the Vikings paint them as peaceful pagan farmers and traders from Scandinavia, given to a little raiding to make ends meet. When they discovered more fruitful lands, they settled and eventually merged with local populations.

Hopefully, Blood-Axe partly redresses the balance. The Vikings certainly emerged from poor Scandinavian farmers fighting each other for their pathetic scrapes of land edged by the freezing seas. Once the power of their warriors and excellence of their ships emerged, this soon changed. The Vikings were fearful and ruthless robbers and slavers, using terror and slaughter to subdue any resistance.

Their skills in combat and martial culture were partly based on the idea that dying in battle led to happiness in Valhalla. The other aspect was extreme mobility. When much of Europe was thick forest, land communication was slow. The splendid Viking long-ships and their ingenious navigation aids allowed long ocean voyages. These were followed by swift passage around coastlines and deep into river systems. They also used stolen horses to fan out from their landing points.

Scandinavian geography led to those from different regions taking separate paths. Those from Jutland invaded the east coast of England and Northern France. Those from what is now Norway invaded Scotland and Ireland before combining with those from Jutland to dominate the entire British Isles. The adventurous moved on to Iceland, Greenland and North America. Those from what is now Sweden traded through the Russian river systems as far as Constantinople and the Black Sea. Their boats were light enough to be manhandled over land for short distances.

Viking raids on Paris led King Charles the Simple to buy them off with grants of land in Normandy in 911. Ragnar Lothbrok's brother Rollo became the ancestor of the Dukes of Normandy.

The Vikings' Norman descendants retained and further developed their ruthless skills in war. Eventually, they conquered the whole of England, along with most of Scotland and Ireland following Duke William's invasion of England in 1066. They also fought around much of the Mediterranean coastline and became rulers of most of Southern Italy and Sicily.

# Spelling of Viking and old English words and names

To add authenticity and a period feel the author has used some old and Viking spellings, rather than modern English versions. The Viking words Jarl for Earl, Konge for King etc. The Old English, Thegn is used instead of the modern variant Thane.

Most of the Viking names used are authentic. Aegea is an exception. She was the queen of the Amazons in Greek legend. They named the Aegean Sea after her.

A conspiracy theorist proposed that my use of Old Norse is part of a Viking plot to move people gradually to speaking the language. Of course, it is.

# Questions for Readers

1. According to a recent survey, the characteristic women most wanted to change in male partners was grumpiness. Are old men worse in this respect? Are they choleric, due to lack of relevance, aches and pains, lost position in society, or other things?

2. Given the changed moral and ethical standards of at least parts of the modern world, are enactments of historic combats healthy? Do they encourage anti-social traits in participants, such as misogyny, racism, racial intolerance, violence and cruelty? Or are they just good clean fun?

3. Are there sizable portions of the populations of major countries to which being a Viking would appeal? How do they satisfy these urges at present? Through which organizations?

4. Does this novel, raise legitimate concerns about cyborgs and robots? How do you feel about their use

5. in sex, war, surveillance, and other aspects of life? What are the possible dangers?

6. Are the reactions of the CIA and British Government to the Vikings as you would expect? If not, how would they differ?

7. Are the strong female characters in this book reflected in real life. Which famous women of past and present might be comparable?

8. Because men behave badly, is it acceptable for women to do the same?

9. Do you think that the incompetence of the police and others shown in reaction to the Vikings is credible? Why, or why not?

10. Can people with empathy and concern for others be drawn into groups such as the Vikings? How could it happen? Has it happened? What about the Mafia, the Nazis, the KKK, ISIS, the major political parties? Can good people be sucked in?

# ABOUT THE AUTHOR

**Brief biography -** Born in the North of England, Chris Clarke has degrees in economics and management. He was a green beret Royal Marine Commando reservist and worked in all the industries mentioned in his books as an Investment Banker and Strategy Consultant. He was latterly CEO and President of a global Executive Search Business headquartered in NY. He and his Scottish wife have worked and lived in Asia, Europe, the US and Latin America.

**Published Fiction -** Chris Clarke has written six previous works of fiction under the name **Aaron Aalborg.** That pen name was suitable for some of his more controversial titles. All are available in e-book and paperback. They are published by Penman House Publishing (http://www.penmanhouse.com) and distributed through Amazon. Blood-Axe is Chris's first novel under his own name.

# WRITTEN AS AARON AALBORG

**They Deserved It** - A historical and contemporary novel, based on a true story about women poisoning their husbands in 17th Century Italy. It is a fast-moving thriller. There is a cast of abused young women, rascally husbands, witches, evil cardinals and a horrible Pope. The discovery of a mysterious Egyptian box moves the story into contemporary New York. There, a rogue lawyer and her lesbian lover, the head of an IT company, continue the murders and are pursued around the world.

**Revolution** - A thrilling account of the assassination of heads of state, including the US President and the British Royal family. It is set in the near future. A socialist revolution and world-wide mayhem follows. The US descends into chaos. There is lots of action and a dramatic twist at the end.

**Doom, Gloom and Despair -** A collection of short

stories including drama around volcanic eruptions, dueling deities and suicidal moments. The stories feature man-eating animals, cannibals and other dark events. Perfect for potential suicides and those of sensitive disposition.

**Cooking the Rich, a post-revolutionary necessity -** This spoof cook book includes hilarious recipes for cooking Donald Trump, The British Royal Family, Rupert Murdoch and many others.

**Terminated - the making of a Serial Killer - volume one - from the slums to the Falklands War -** In this thriller Alex, a poor boy from Scotland and martial artist, beats the odds to win a top education. He becomes a successful businessman. Recruited by a crack special services unit, he is embroiled in the Falklands War with Argentina. He returns a hero. There is non-stop excitement. His personal life is also dramatic.

**Terminated - the making of a Serial Killer - volume two - from hero to serial killer -** Alex returns to a stellar international business career. He soon becomes embroiled in the evils of the business world. He meets psychopaths in politics, top management consulting and investment banking. After murders and assassinations, he becomes CEO of an Executive Search firm. He discovers that headhunting is as corrupt as everything else. After trying to fight his demons in a Buddhist monastery, he returns like an avenging angel to eliminate those he feels deserve it.

# Writing as Chris Clarke and Planned for 2018

**Save the Bonsai -** A jaded computer hacker and serial activist is disillusioned with too many silly causes. As a joke, he starts a spoof movement, "Save the Bonsai." These sad little trees are twisted and tortured for perverse pleasure by uncaring humanity. To his surprise, the idea becomes a runaway success. A terrorist wing, The Bonsai Liberation Army, causes him to become a hunted fugitive.

He flees, but ends in the hands of a sinister Japanese professor of genetic engineering who is developing carnivorous plants. The ending is unexpected and dramatic.

# By K. Francis Ryan

## A Penman House Author

### The Echoes Quartet

**Echoes Through the Mist** –

Book I in the Echoes Quartet

Julian Blessing is rescued from a life on Wall Street that is killing him. He possesses extraordinary paranormal abilities—abilities he doesn't realize he has until he is confronted by madness and evil on the rocky coast of Ireland.

**Echoes Through the Vatican** –

Book II in the Echoes Quartet

Greed, corruption, money laundering and murder—that's what awaits Julian Blessing in The Eternal City. Rome is Julian's destination, but often the reasons we go somewhere are not the reasons we need to be there. Then there is the Jesuit Book. It is a book that shouldn't exist, that many hope doesn't exist and that people will kill to possess.

**Echoes from the Past** –

Book III in the Echoes Quartet

Julian Blessing is back on Ireland's fog-cloaked coast. He has to build up his paranormal defenses if he hopes to protect an age-old treasure. Faltering in his mission will bring chaos to the world and everything Julian holds dearer than his life will be lost.

**Echoes Through Time** –

Book IV in the Echoes Quartet [currently in writing]

Julian Blessing has returned to the peaceful village of Cappel Vale. Below the surface however a secret is harbored—a secret that involves a heinous crime from the distant past and its present-day punishment. The criminal has been found, sentence has been passed, but protecting identity of the executioner is essential to the welfare of the village.

An evil from Julian's past has returned for revenge. Failure to expunge the malevolence will cost Julian everything and everyone he loves.

www.ingramcontent.com/pod-product-compliance
Lightning Source LLC
Chambersburg PA
CBHW070815120626
46556CB00002B/509